Nell Didn't Do It

Was it Nell's best friend, Alice?

"I know what goes on in there," the angry mom said, screeching at the world.

"You people have been making hash oil and now your lab has exploded."

The Soon-to-be ex-Husband Wanted Money

"Has something come up? Have you heard from Max?"

"I worry about you Nell, the way he left you high and dry."

I nodded, but didn't believe him. There was something more, something left unsaid. A subtle warning about Max, a warning to prepare for another encounter.

There Is More Nell Letterly
And More Sue Star!

***Murder in the Dojo* (#1 in the Nell Letterly Series):** The book that started it all.

***Murder with Altitude* (#2):** A training run turns deadly.

***Murder by Moose* (#4) Coming in 2017:** Autumn treks in high-mountain meadows sometimes lead to murder.

Available in trade paper and e-book format.

Also Enjoy Sue's Short Story Collections
About Other Strong Women and Nell's Friends

Organized Death: Even organized women stumble when a crime occurs.
Trophy Hunting: Trophies come in all forms.
Trouble in a Politically Correct Town: Nell's friends battle the powers that be.

Available as e-books for all e-readers.
Read selections at: dmkregpublishing.com

Murder for a Cash Crop

Sue Star

D. M. Kreg Publishing

DMKregPublishing.com

Cover Design: Renee Barratt, The Cover Counts

For Al, without whom this book would not exist.

Acknowledgments

Thanks to the many fine martial artists with whom I've trained, and especially thanks to Mr. Reid. Thanks also to the writers who helped this project along the way: the Boulder Lunch Bunch, who first encouraged me to write about Nell; the Inklings, my awesome critique group; the Oregon Writers Network, whose support keeps my career on track; and my first readers who re-arranged their schedules to accomodate mine. Thanks to my family for always humoring me and believing in me. Thanks also to my editor, Lyn Worthen and to my publisher, Donald Kreg. This book wouldn't have happened without any of you.

Murder for a Cash Crop

Sue Star

One

A WHIFF OF WEED floated through the open windows of the karate studio.

I'd cranked the windows open and propped open both front and back doors to let the cooling air of twilight circulate through our stifling workout space. It was a hollowed-out hundred-year-old converted bungalow, which of course didn't have air conditioning. I didn't want my students to pass out from the buildup of searing heat of late summer, a heat so intense that it could bake the air and poof it into dust. Now the breeze swirled its powdery grit, along with that distinctively indefinable, yet unmistakably tangy smell.

Pot.

Sort of like a combination of used shoes and burning incense.

Pot was legal in Boulder and all of Colorado. Some thought it was nirvana, others thought it was evil incarnate. I just thought it was a poor substitute for meditation.

Of course, I didn't have experience with any stimulants other than meditation and heavy martial arts.

I tried to ignore the reminder of someone's party nearby.

Bone-tired and past my bedtime, I was already having enough trouble focusing on my students. Seven hotshot tweens and teens, all belt levels, were jumping and whirling and kicking and punching before me in their sweat-soaked T-shirts. It was after the last class of the day, and they were using this time to choreograph an upcoming performance for an end-of-summer festival. The casualness of the night combined with the heat of summer gave all of us privileges to wear only our loose, cotton karate trousers and T-shirts rather than full *gi*.

With the drifting smell, my students couldn't focus any better than I could. Punching arms dropped. Bare feet landed in sloppy stances. Their faces contorted into dramatic sniffing spasms, as if they were imitating hound dogs. One of the girls covered her mouth and giggled. They twisted this way and that, searching for the pot smoker.

Then one of them, squeaky-wheel Elliott, pointed at the window behind me and yelped.

We all turned to gape at the mullioned panes that overlooked the side yard jungle, shadowed with thickening nightfall and overgrown junipers. Through the blistering glass, I saw a spot of red-orange flicker against the dark. From its angle through the trees, I could tell it was coming from an upper window of Alice's Victorian house next door.

"Fire!" Several voices shouted at the same time.

"Oh no no no!" Mumbling sounds slipped out of me as I froze in place. Or maybe it was my heart clenching in my chest. I glanced over to the folding chairs near the front door where parents often sat to observe classes, but tonight none had come. I was the only adult in the room.

"My sister's over there!" Elliott choked on his words, and the despair in his voice snapped me out of my momentary freeze.

I whirled around and ninja-dashed across the workout floor, heading toward the office phone at the back of the studio. It was closer than my cell phone, which was upstairs in my apartment. I hadn't made it very far before footsteps thudded up the porch steps out front and clattered across the wooden floor of the entry hall. I spun around, in sort of a sloppy tornado kick without the kick, and recognized the young woman as Elliott's sister, Robinette. She often picked up Elliott after class. Now a feral look glazed her flushed face as she ran onto the workout floor, gasping.

"Help! Call for help!"

"Robi!" Elliott cried. "What's wrong?"

"There's a fire," she said, pausing to suck air. "I think someone's trapped inside. You've got to help." Wisps of white-blonde hair fringed the kohl rings around her eyes, adding to her wild and frenzied look.

"On my way," I said, leaping down the twisting hall toward my office. I could move pretty fast for a middle-aged mom.

What we used for an office had been the kitchen when this bungalow was someone's home back in the day. The only phone in this place was located back there. I'd tried to persuade my boss, Arlo Callahan, to install an extension on the workout floor — the former living and dining rooms — but no dice. He was an even bigger Luddite than me.

I reached for the clunky yellow phone, inherited along with autumn gold kitchen appliances, and dialed 9-1-1 to the ripping sounds of zippers and Velcro. The first of my students had untwisted themselves from their gawking positions at the window and managed to scramble toward the racks where they stowed their bags and their cell phones. For any workout on the floor, I made my students shed their phones, silence them, or better yet, turn them off. They complied because they all knew that at the first peep of a phone, I would confiscate it.

With all the calls I've made these last few months, I should set up an account with 9-1-1, I thought lamely as the dispatcher ran me through the usual procedure. My name was Nell Letterly, I told her. I knew the operator was only doing her job, but really. Could we get on with the emergency?

Finally, after I told her the nature of my emergency, she assured me that the fire had already been reported. She could've said that at the outset and saved me a few more gray hairs. I glanced around the curve of the hall, but from my position, anchored by the cord—yes, an actual phone cord—chaining me to my desk, I couldn't see my students. I heard the buzz of their chatter, instead. Surely, none of them had managed to get through to dispatch before me.

I did not know the extent of the fire next door at Alice's Arts and Crafts Shoppe. Alice, my new best friend, liked to spell it "shoppe," not shop, because it was a special, magical place. Her words, not mine.

Oh dear, I hoped Alice wasn't the person trapped inside.

Actually, I hoped *no* one was trapped inside. How bad was the fire if it had trapped someone? All I had seen was one flame, shooting out of an upper-floor window. Although, that was probably not a good sign. If the fire had reached the upper floors, then didn't that mean the fire was pretty much consuming the entire house? It must be spreading like wildfire. No wonder that cliché meant speed.

And all that separated my studio from Alice's *shoppe* was a side yard filled with kindling.

It wouldn't take much in this dry climate, at this driest time of year—wildfire season—for a fire to spread. One gust of wind—and we had lots of wind hurling down the side of the mountains here along the front range—could carry a burning cinder across the twenty-yard distance to my roof. Before anyone knew it, this building would be engulfed, too.

Time to corral my students. I was responsible for them as well as the martial arts studio.

I dropped the phone and ran back down the hall to the workout floor, where my seven students huddled around the bag rack with cell phones pressed to their ears.

"The fire department is on the way," I told them, trying to inject calm authority into my voice in spite of my hammering pulse rate. "We'll stay together until your parents arrive."

In case we need to evacuate.

I hadn't said it, but they must've read my mind. They charged, squealing, toward the foyer and squeezed through the bottleneck of the front door.

"Hold on!" I yelled, sprinting after them.

Outside, the smoke singed my lungs, and I felt as if I couldn't breathe. My students stood rooted in place along the tilting cracks of the sidewalk. Overhead, cottonwoods—the hanging trees from the old west—rattled their leaves in the breeze that tossed Alice's flames about, licking for purchase to spread.

There were only six students.

One of them, an orange belt named Chanel, who was the most dedicated and diligent of this bunch, making up for her deficiency in athletic talent, broke away from the group and scurried over to me. "I couldn't stop him!" she said amidst choking sobs.

"Who?" I scanned the huddle. Elliott was missing. So was his sister.

"He said..." Chanel gasped. "He had to... had to... stop Robinette. She went back inside, looking for that person she said is trapped over there, and Elliott followed her!"

My heart froze, in spite of the outdoor furnace blasting my face. I scanned the thickening crowd of curious rubber neckers. Light leaked out from the neighbors' open doorways and the flames from Alice's house, illuminating this sloping block of off-campus university terrain known as the Hill. Hundred-year-old bungalows had been converted into student rentals with a mix of commercial that catered to the pleasures and needs of twenty-somethings.

I didn't see either Elliott or his older sister.

Chanel stared at the burning building. Her freckled face had gone pasty pale, and her freckles stood out. "I couldn't stop him. I tried, but I couldn't!" Her lower lip quivered, and she covered her face with her hands.

I hugged her close. "Try not to worry, honey. We'll get them out of there safe. It's not your fault."

I shouldn't call my students by such endearing terms, but I couldn't help being a mom. That's what I was. My fifteen-year-old daughter should be home any minute from her band practice. Where was Terra? It looked as if the rest of tonight's demo prep was canceled. We didn't even have a chance to bow out properly.

Maybe we were canceled forever, if that fire spread.

Nell, Nell, Master Hwang's chiding voice rang in my head. *Clear your mind of negative thinking.*

I know, I know, but it was true. If we burned down... Then

what? Not even my master sensei could find the hidden strength to overcome such a fate.

"Stay here," I told my students. I gave Chanel an encouraging squeeze and rushed up the incline of the hill toward the burning house. The sound of a siren's wail drifted like sweet music to my ears.

Good grief. Elliott's sister was an adult. Why on earth would she have led her little brother inside a burning building?

I reached the porch steps of Alice's house as the fire truck turned a corner and wailed closer. The front door stood open, revealing an eerie, orangish, backlit interior. "Elliott!" I called into the roiling smoke, hot as a furnace. Crackling and snapping sounds made my stomach feel sick. "Alice!"

As I debated the wisdom of plunging inside, two figures burst out from the inferno, out onto the porch. Thank goodness! Elliott and Robinette stumbled across the porch, and I raced up there to help drag them down the steps and onto the grass.

But where was Alice?

My squeaky-wheel student, Elliott, a brave runt of a kid, wiped away the kohl smudges streaking down his sister's cheeks. They coughed, and the young woman cried as I bent over them, making soothing sounds. Coughing was a good thing, right? It meant they were breathing.

"Do you realize what you did, you twerp?" Robinette shoved Elliott's hands away from her face. She gulped back tears and choked, struggling to stand. "I would've gotten to him if you hadn't dragged me out first." She made a move back towards the house.

"You're not going back in there." I clamped my fingers tight around her skinny wrist, scarcely bigger than the rubber flail of my practice chuks—nunchaku. If she thought she was heading into a burning building, she would have to get past me first. And past Elliott, who leapt to his sister's other side and blocked her from running back into the burning house.

The fire truck screeched into position, and suited-up firefighters jumped down from the truck. One of them swished and jingled in our direction, as much as his suit would allow him to move. "Is everyone okay here?" he yelled at me as his colleagues hooked up their hoses.

"I think so," I called, waving him back to his duties, "but I don't know where Alice is." My voice quivered.

"*She's* not the problem," Robinette wailed. "She went to the movies tonight. It's that other guy. The artist."

I felt the blood drain from my face as I suddenly remembered Alice's renter. "He rents studio space from Alice! Where is *he*?" I had never met him, but occasionally I had seen the artist—Felix Something—come and go. Alice had told me he rented studio space from her because her Victorian house had an honest-to-gosh garret. I had even seen him outside a couple times, painting weird alley stuff that his artist's eye claimed were *objets d'art* in the trash-can lined alley that ran behind our buildings.

"Maybe he's not in there after all," Robinette said. "I thought he was, and I called out, but no one answered. I heard a noise, and I thought it was him, but maybe I was wrong."

"There's a cat." Elliott's voice rose to a whine. "Remember, Robi? You told me how the cat is always getting into paint, 'cause it's a Siamese, and it's—"

"Gotcha." The firefighter lurched over to one of his partners, consulted briefly with him, although you couldn't tell if any of them was a him or a her on account of their bulky suits, and then two of them charged past us, up the walk, clanking toward the front door.

Another of the firefighters helping hook up the hoses shouted at us. "Ambulance on the way."

"Ambulance?" Robinette said with a cough. She looked dazed, as if she'd just woken up from a bad dream. "No! Not for me! I don't need an ambulance."

"We just need the paramedics to check you out, ma'am."

Robinette sobbed and twisted around in her brother's and my restraints to stare at the craft shoppe. Flames crackled out of an upper window. The attic garret. An arching spray of water hissed, swiping across the brick front of the house.

Just then, a woman's scream ripped through the gathering crowd on the sidewalk. Curious onlookers jumped to either side as a tall, thin woman torpedoed her way through them and shouted, "My house! That's my house!"

Alice.

I released Robinette to Elliott's care and ran to Alice's side, encircling her in my arms. I whispered soothing sounds and stroked her trembling arms. Her soft weight collapsed against me, infusing me with the heat of her flushed body. Holding her up, I steered her to a patch of straw-dried grass just beyond the range of the crowd.

"Everyone get back!" one of the firefighters yelled. The hoses bucked in their arms as water hissed, smacking against bricks and dousing the flames.

A dark, stout man in the crowd appointed himself policeman and herded most of the gawkers across the street, giving the firefighters space to do their job. I tugged at Alice to come with me to the karate studio next door, but she wouldn't budge.

"My house!" Alice twisted out of my grip and wailed. Her fingers spasmed in and out of fists and clawed at loose strands of her reddish golden hair, sparkling in the fire's glow. One lopsided tail fell free of its pins. "What have you done to my house?"

"Can you get them out of the way?" one of the firefighters asked, dipping his helmeted head at me.

"Felix! Did he do this?" Alice thrashed, pushing one way and then the other, scanning the crowd for Felix.

"Ma'am, help us out here?" the firefighter said to me again, brusquely this time.

I obliged. "Come on." I tightened my fingers on Alice's arms and guided her forcefully down the hill in the direction of the karate studio. I nodded at Elliott to do the same for Robinette. "We're all going to wait next door, while the professionals do their job."

Not that I was sure the karate studio would be any safer, not if that fire spread. We staggered next door as Alice continued to gasp and Robinette sobbed. Elliott and I gently pushed the two women down onto the steps leading up to my front porch. Chanel and the rest of the students clustered around us, edging closer.

"What happened?" several of them said in unison.

Alice mumbled, as if in a trance. "No... It can't be happening... Not again..."

I nodded at the nearest student. "Go get them some water." The student ran inside.

Neighbors—university students mostly, since this older residential section of the town bordered the university's gown— trickled across the street, gathering in clumps. Some of them strolled along the sidewalk and joined my students' huddle.

"You know when that started?"

"No, I just got here…"

"Is everyone okay?"

"No, they think there might be someone inside…"

"Oh, man… Anything we can do to help?"

Parents came and went, collecting their children and shuffling them away. But not Elliott's. He explained, because Robinette couldn't, that his sister worked part-time for Alice. Long story short, she had brought him to karate because she wanted to clock some work time next door while he was at practice. His parents never intended to pick him up. Robinette was responsible for taking her brother home. She was the adult. But the way she broke down and sobbed, and the way he took care of her, their roles seemed to have reversed.

Above the din of curiosity seekers rose one voice, growing more and more querulous. "I bet I can guess what started all this." It was a woman. Sarcasm oozed from her tone of voice.

Her animosity made me rise to all five feet of my height and turn to face her. I recognized her as one of the permanent neighbors, not a student renter. In her late thirties, I thought, she must come from a block or two away, somewhere farther up the hill. I'd seen her pushing a baby stroller past the studio, presumably on her way to the bus stop. She was a stay-at-home mom with young children and a husband who supported them. The kids weren't with her now. Hopefully, they were home with their dad. This woman was as out-of-place in this neighborhood as I was. I'd never talked to her though, so I never realized before just how full of anger she was.

"I know what goes on in there," the angry mom said,

screeching at the world and steaming with garlicky breath in my face.

Alice sprang up from the porch steps. Robinette looked up from her tear and kohl sodden hands that had been covering her face. Alice edged close to my side, practically attaching to my hip. The angle of her chin jutted out. I'd seen that same defiant look on my teenager.

The neighbor mom stuck her finger in Alice's face. "You people have been making hash oil in there all along, that's what. And now your lab exploded."

Gasps swept through the air, or maybe it was the roar of the fire.

"Shut up!" Alice screamed back. She grabbed the mom's finger and shook it. They looked like they were arm wrestling, only with fingers. "Just shut your friggin' mouth!"

Nearby onlookers buzzed among themselves.

"Alice!" I stepped between the two women and grabbed their locked fingers, prying them apart. The neighborhood mom yanked free of me. Her arm snapped away from me like a slingshot.

I put my arm around Alice and rubbed her back. Spine knobs bristled like armor. My soothing efforts didn't calm her down. It was as if the fire had heated her up to this new level of agitation. I'd never heard her swear before. I'd never even heard her raise her voice before.

Alice shook me off and charged after the neighborhood mom, matching her anger with a fury of her own. "Who do you think you are, talking to me that way? You don't know squat! How dare you accuse me of something like that? Hash oil? Are you serious?"

The mom took a step backwards, as if retreating from the range of Alice's lashing. "Why not? You use your store as a front for marijuana sales. You don't even have a license. I'm here to tell you, it's ruining the neighborhood. See what happened?"

"Maybe we can sit down and talk and sort this all out," I said in my unruffled voice, trying to emulate my sensei's calm.

"No, Nell," Alice said. "She's way past talking."

"Let's be sensible —"

The neighbor mom turned to me with her pointing finger. "And as for *you*." Pure loathing coated her words. "It's always something, isn't it? All spring and summer it's been the police, and now it's the fire department. Are you like a magnet for trouble or what?"

Whoa. I cringed from the reek of her negativity. As if it was my fault the house next door was burning.

"You can't talk to my friend like that, either," Alice said. "Your complaint is with me, not her, so let's have it."

The mom reached past me and grabbed a fistful of Alice's loose hair tail. She tugged, bringing down the rest of Alice's do, and Alice swore again, swatting at the mom's arm. They were fighting all wrong. Arms flailed wildly, leaving their midsections temptingly unprotected. I thought about inserting a couple of well-placed kicks there, just enough to take their breaths away, but I didn't want to accidentally hurt them.

"Stop it," I said, timing my moves like a kid entering a twirling jumprope. I stepped closer, reaching for their swinging arms. A bad move.

And I was too slow. A fist popped me in the nose.

"Oh!" I touched the stinging spot. The nose was still there.

Elliott yelped. "Ms. Letterly! Are you okay?"

"Omigod! You're hurt!" Alice gasped and turned her attention away from the mom.

Flailing, swinging arms dropped. The neighborhood mom shrank away from us, fading into the crowd. Someone's camera flash went off in my face, blinding me.

"Nell!" Alice shouted again, but I wasn't deaf. "Say something!"

"We should enroll you in lessons," I said, gingerly poking at my face. A warm wetness tickled inside my nose, as if it was trying to make up its mind to bleed or not.

Alice sobbed and moaned. "I'm so, so sorry." I'd meant for her to laugh, to release some tension, not to cry harder.

"No worries," I said. "It's not even bleeding. But I should be prepared, just in case. Elliott, can you run inside and get me a towel?"

He scampered away, up the porch steps, and Alice snatched her purse from where she'd dropped it beside Robinette. "Wait, I have a tissue in my purse." She dug around inside and produced a wad of tissues, which I pressed against my nose.

Murmurs arose from the crowd of onlookers, and more camera flashes sparked the night. There was movement at the front door of Alice's burning house. The two firefighters who'd gone inside looking for Felix burst outside. Between them, they carried someone's inert body and laid it down gently on the grass.

"Felix!" Alice shouted, lurching away from me. I sprang after her and grabbed her arm, keeping her from bolting up the hill.

Robinette's small voice squeaked. "Is he...is he dead?"

Two

WAS HE? Was Felix dead?

That's all I could think about as time passed. Alice's incoherent mutterings sounded as if she was more preoccupied about her house, than about Felix. Out on the street, the night filled with flashing lights of cop cars and emergency vehicles. An ambulance came and went, carrying Felix away. Gawkers came and also went. The angry neighborhood mom disappeared. Light bulbs flashed against the night sky, catching sprays of water. As the fire simmered down and fizzled out, Terra returned home, sputtering her disbelief that she'd missed the action. Soggy blankets of dark smoke wisped from the windows.

Alice's house still stood, but it was a darkened, charred shell.

Then my dad pushed his way through the lingering onlookers. He was dressed in his houseslippers and terrycloth robe. "I came as soon as I heard on the scanner, Nellie," he said.

"Dad, you don't have a scanner."

"I do now. Bought it at Wal-Mart. If you insist on living this way in this Tom-fool place, then I want to know right away whenever there's trouble around you."

Seeing the tight set of his jaw, I knew where we were going

to be spending the rest of the night. Sometimes there's no use arguing with your dad. So Alice, Terra, Samurai Q. Ferret and I piled into Dad's pick-up truck, and he drove us in stony silence five miles east of Boulder to his compact, three-acre farm.

None of us wanted to talk about it in front of Alice.

We were all burning to talk about it.

Dad gave Alice his guestroom and a brand-new toothbrush. She drifted inside with nothing but the clothes on her back and the purse she'd carried with her to the movies, and she closed the door behind her. The click of the lock told the rest of us that she was done for the night.

We weren't.

Dad, Terra, and I headed to the linoleum table in his 'fifties style kitchen for a nightcap. In other words, ice cream for Terra, a splash of bourbon for Dad (it helped him sleep, he claimed), and peppermint tea for me. Along with an ice pack for my nose.

"Wow," Terra said with each clink of her spoon. "Now I can't go to band camp in the morning."

"You bet your sweet bippy you can," Dad said before I could interject a single word. "I'll drive you, no matter what kind of heck-fire your so-called friend drags you through."

I interrupted fast. "Alice *is* our friend, Dad, and she's been good to me. I can't abandon her now."

He snorted and threw some more bourbon down his throat. "Nellie, you know what your problem is?"

Terra's spoon stilled while I stirred and stirred, even though the honey had already dissolved in my tea.

Dad went on. "You always did feel too sorry for every Tom, Dick, and Harry. Lemme tell you, if there was ever a stray cat on the road, we could always count on you to drag it inside."

26

"Consistency is the key to life." Truth be told, my dad was the one who'd always kept a saucer of fresh milk in the barn for those stray cats roaming through.

"What do you really know about this woman, anyway?" Dad narrowed his eyes and sniffed the swirling golden contents that sloshed around inside his jelly jar.

"She's been my friend since we moved into the karate studio last March."

He snorted. "What else?"

"She came here from California."

"So do three fourths of all the danged newcomers."

I knew Dad's negative opinion about the population explosion in our hometown. "You'd like her. She has a green thumb."

He stopped swirling his drink and looked up at me.

Encouraged, I went on. "She tends a vegetable garden in that patch of space between her house and the alley. Tomatoes, beans, lettuce, and I don't know what all. You should see it, Dad. So one time I laughingly invited her to come over and tend my patch of weeds, and wouldn't you know? She took me up on it."

"You mean, she sprayed your weeds with Roundup?"

"Heck no, Dad, she's as green as her thumb."

He grumbled. "Good. Another transplanted liberal who speaks green. We don't have enough of 'em in town. What made her come here? Marijuana, I'll bet."

"Shhhh, lower your voice. She'll hear you."

He raised his voice. "Nellie, clean out your ears. I heard the talk among those looky-loo neighbors of yours. That's what they was saying. She deals marijuana and who knows what else on the side, and it blew up. You better watch yourself with that one."

27

"First of all, Dad, she moved into that house several years ago, before marijuana was legalized." I set down my ice pack and held up one hand to waggle a finger to tick off my points. "And secondly, it was Chief Niwot's curse that brought her here."

Dad grunted and chugged more bourbon. "That's a Tomfool excuse if I ever heard it. Mighty convenient, too, for all the newcomers to use."

I shrugged, noncommittal, and repositioned the ice pack. Chief Niwot's curse was a local legend that explained why those who'd moved away from town ended up coming back. They couldn't help themselves, on account of the curse, which made them return. "Alice spent some time here one summer when she was still in school, fifteen years ago, or so. She always wanted to come back. Then, about five years ago, maybe more, she answered an ad to become a companion to an elderly lady who had lived all her life in that lovely house—the one that burned tonight."

My voice choked, thinking of the destruction of such charm, not to mention history. I hoped the house could be restored. The damage was extensive, no doubt, but the brick construction should have withstood the worst of it.

"The old lady—Mrs. Harris—didn't have any family, and when she died, she left the house and its contents to Alice. That's when Alice decided to open the craft shoppe."

"What? No trust fund?"

"Your sarcasm is not appreciated," I said, glaring at the bottle. He always preferred the cheap brand, a difficult find here in Boulder.

It was the bourbon speaking for him tonight. And it told me loud and clear just how rattled Dad was by how close the fire disaster had come to *me*. His crusty veneer always showed when he was scared. I stood up, screwed the cap back onto the bottle, and shoved it into the cabinet above the refrigerator.

"Nellie, you're just like your mother, y'know it?"

"Good night, Dad."

"What's this world coming to? Someone's got to look out for you, now your mother's gone."

Good *night*, Dad."

Terra and I would bunk on the two sofas in the living room—a newer one, and the old one Mother had picked out way back when they were newlyweds. When it had come time for Dad to buy a new sofa, he simply moved the old one back to a far corner of the room, behind the new furniture. He couldn't bear to part with it. I headed into the living room and spread out Mother's quilts, tucking them in and around the cushions on both sofas. After Mother's death from breast cancer, her sofa remained his link to her. He'd lost Mother; he couldn't lose the physical reminders of her, too, even though the couch had sprouted sprung springs.

They dug into my back all night.

But the sprung springs weren't the reason I tossed and turned the rest of the night. It was about the artist. Felix. Was he still alive? Or had he passed in the night?

And what had Alice meant when she'd moaned, *No... It can't be happening... Not again...* Did that mean she'd lost a house to fire before? The poor woman!

"Mom?" Terra whispered at me from her sofa. "Are you still awake?"

I murmured affirmatively.

"Was Gramps right? About the marijuana and all? What's

gonna happen now?"

"Sweetie, I wish I knew. For starters, Alice will move in with us."

"Do I have to give up my *room*? I just got it fixed up the way I want it."

I sighed. I hadn't asked Terra about all the changes I'd imposed on her life in the last year. I'd just told her how it was going to be. I'd had to. Because her dad—the louse—had left us, with no warning. One day he just walked away, rejecting not only me but Terra, too. We'd had to leave our fancy house in the suburbs, the only home Terra had ever known, to go live in the apartment above the studio. Her new room was the one small pleasure she'd managed to find in all this mess.

"No, honey, you get to keep your room."

Sammy poked her head out from under Terra's quilt and scolded me with ferret chitters.

"What, not getting your beauty sleep?" I said with a chuckle. "Night, night."

Terra would keep her room. She needed it. But where would I put Alice in the three-room apartment above the karate studio?

* * * * *

In the morning, we lined up for use of the one bathroom. The usual order in Dad's farmhouse, when it was just Terra and me staying overnight, was Dad got to use the bathroom first, followed by me, and the teenager always came last, who could then spend as much time doing whatever it was that teenagers did to tie up bathrooms. But this morning Alice was the guest, so she got the bathroom first. While she was in there, Dad lurked in the hall, waiting his turn.

I slipped outside and crunched down the gravel driveway for the newspaper. It promised to be another scorcher today, and I quickly headed back inside. In the hall along the way to the kitchen, I had to pass the guestroom. Its door stood open, revealing the forlornly empty room. The bedcovers were rumpled, and Alice's purse sat on the table next to the bed. That was all she had left in the world. No suitcase. No change of clothes. My heart ached a little more for her.

Dad wanted to make flapjacks this morning. He loved showing off his flipping skills, especially to unsuspecting guests. I got the batter started, between glances at the front page photo of last night's fire. I wasn't much of a cook, but I could at least follow directions on a box of mix.

"How are you feeling this morning?" I said when Dad finally dragged himself out of the bathroom. My gaze drifted toward the cupboard above the refrigerator.

"Slept like a baby," he said with a wink, and then snapped the newspaper open in front of his face.

"I wish I could say the same for myself," I mumbled.

"Nellie, there's nothing like a good old-fashioned shot of medicine. You'd better put more ice on that nose of yours."

"It's not so bad. I don't think it's going to turn into a black eye this time."

He grunted.

Terra walked into the kitchen just then and poked behind the door where Dad kept a broom. "Has anyone seen Sammy?"

"I thought she was with you. Last I saw her, she was snuggled in the covers with you."

"That was hours ago. She must be exploring."

"Uh-oh." I didn't like it when Sammy explored. She had a habit of collecting shiny things and stashing them into hiding places. Although I didn't think she was familiar enough with Dad's place that she kept a nest of her collections here.

"Lemme in there," Dad said, throwing down the paper when it was clear I'd finished mixing the batter and was just stalling. He took the stick of butter from my hands and dropped a chunk to sizzle on the griddle.

We stood back and watched him expertly flip the hotcakes in the air while we drooled over the buttery aromas.

I glanced at the paper and thought of Felix. I hoped he was alert enough this morning to enjoy breakfast in the hospital, as much as the venue and his reason for being there could provide enjoyment. "I'm going to call the hospital to find out how that artist is doing this morning," I said to no one in particular. Dad was busy transferring hotcakes to plates that Terra held.

"Let him suffer," Alice said, entering the kitchen. "He deserves it."

I wanted to hug her, to welcome her back from her shock. Joining the conversation was a good sign, despite the anger in her voice. "What do you mean?" I asked.

"If it was his absent-mindedness that caused this fire, I'm gonna kill him."

"Not really?" I was more stunned about the fact that her words streamed freely, rather than the content of what she said. "Absent-minded, is he?"

Had there been any truth to the angry neighbor's claim of hash oil? I rejected the thought as fast as it flashed through my mind. Still... Had something disoriented Felix enough the night before that he'd become trapped in the fire? Good thing the firefighters got to him so fast.

Alice apparently had a similar thought, as her tone of voice lowered to a growl. "He probably left one of his artist lights plugged in where it shouldn't have been, up there in his attic. If they find out it was a short, or faulty wiring, or something that could've started that fire, I'm gonna kill him. Just as soon as he recovers."

"That woman last night thought the fire started from hash oil. Do you think that's what he was doing?"

Alice sighed. "Honestly, I don't know what to think. Felix never allowed anyone upstairs, except for his friend Dominic. That was his private domain. He rented out the entire upper level, and I always respected his wish for privacy, even if he wasn't always timely with his rent money."

"Don't worry. If he's as absent-minded as all that, he wouldn't have had the wherewithal to do anything he shouldn't have been doing."

Alice sighed. "I hope you're right. But still—"

"It's all water under the bridge now," Dad pointed out.

"You're right, Mr. Letterly," Alice said. "And besides, it was supposed to be a privilege and an honor that he chose to rent from *me* and operate his studio in my place. He was very famous. He had a waiting list of students who wanted to take class with him, and the cost was outrageously high. Their coming through the shoppe was good traffic for me."

Was? He wasn't dead, after all.

Dad dropped his spatula, clattering onto the Formica countertop. "I don't know, Nellie. Maybe you'd better think twice about that job of yours. It puts you smack in the middle of the marijuana industry."

"There's nothing illegal going on in my house, Mr. Letterly," Alice said, balling one of her hands into a fist. Her voice rose. "Felix is just a stereotypical absent-minded artist. What I sell—sold—in my shoppe is all perfectly legal."

"Of course it's legal," I said, trying to soothe her. "Da-a-ad," I said, throwing him an evil eye glare over my shoulder.

"Let's eat," Terra said, brilliantly knowing how to change the topic of conversation. "I'm starving."

"You go ahead and start on the first batch. I need to phone the hospital. I'll be there in time for the next batch." I needed to know about Felix's condition before I could enjoy any food. "What's Felix's last name?"

"Todd," Alice said. "Felix Todd."

The woman who answered the phone at the other end, at the hospital, asked me to hold while she looked up the patient. "I'm sorry," she said, coming back on the line a short while later. "We have no patient by that name."

My insides quivered. That didn't sound good. "But I saw the ambulance drive away with him."

"Are you sure they brought him to this hospital and not to one of the others servicing the metro area?"

No I wasn't sure. "But your hospital is the closest one to us." I didn't like not being sure. I didn't like whining, either. My life as a martial artist was a no-whine zone.

"That doesn't necessarily mean that your friend would've been brought here. It depends on who his doctor is."

That didn't make sense, not for an emergency. "Actually, he's not a friend. I don't know Felix, not personally. He was in that house fire last night at Alice's craft shoppe. Up on the Hill." I gave her the address. "Wasn't the victim of that fire brought to

34

the hospital?" I didn't want to hear what I feared: he wasn't in the hospital because he was in the morgue.

"Oh! Well, why didn't you say so in the first place? The patient you're talking about, the one who suffered smoke inhalation from that fire? He's doing just fine this morning and should be released later today. His name, by the way, isn't Felix Todd. It is Jackson James."

The phone slipped out of my hand and fell with a thud to Dad's linoleum floor. I scrabbled around the floor, chasing the phone, but only managed to slide it across the slick floor, spinning just beyond my reach, as it finally came to rest under Mother's colonial highboy.

"Hello? Hello?" I could hear the voice of the hospital receptionist on the other end of the line.

By the time I reached under the furniture, through cobwebs and past dust bunnies, and retrieved the phone, the receptionist had hung up. Just as well. My own voice was in no condition to speak coherently. It was hard to believe she was talking about *my* Jackson James—one of my soon-to-be-ex husband's colleagues at the university. Maybe there were other people with that same name in this town. More importantly, how on earth had Jackson James come to be the victim of smoke inhalation in Alice's fire? What had he been doing inside Alice's burning shoppe to be dragged outside by firefighters?

Three

NO LONGER HUNGRY, I went through the motions of eating Dad's flapjacks. I did not taste them. My stomach twisted in knots.

If the victim from the fire had been Jackson James—my husband's pal, Jack—then it begged more questions.

Like, where was Felix Todd?

Alice seemed even more upset. She said Felix must've gone away overnight, maybe scouting out plein air sites. Sometimes he did that on weekends. But the problem with that theory was that it wasn't a weekend.

Terra searched for Sammy while I washed up the breakfast dishes. She finally pulled the ferret out from under the guest bed, and then we all piled into Dad's truck. Driving west into town, we fought traffic all the way. No one—except the wealthy California transplants—could afford to buy a house inside the city limits anymore, not with its skyrocketing costs, especially not with the lure of more affordable satellite communities within a ten-mile radius. That created havoc on the roads at rush hour. Fortunately, Terra's band camp started a lazy half-hour after the main crunch of rush hour had died down.

"How could we have mistaken Felix for Jackson James?"

37

I said to no one in particular, shaking my head. "When the firefighters brought him out last night?"

"It was dark," Alice said softly from the back seat.

"But they don't look anything alike." I sputtered and twisted around in my seat to face her. "They're polar opposites. Jackson is so refined, and Felix is...I don't know..."

"Sloppy?"

"You said it, not me. But the truth is, I never saw him come and go without a paint-smeared shirt."

"Exactly."

"Someone should've noticed."

"If you recall, you wouldn't let me go to him, remember?"

"Sure. It was still a fire scene, and they didn't want us in their way. I'd like to know what Jackson was doing there in the first place. And where Felix is."

Alice didn't answer. Her eyes teared up. She opened her mouth as if she wanted to speak, but words didn't come out.

Dad's attention flicked from the road to the rear-view mirror, and then to me. "Nellie, don't you go on like that."

I watched the road for him until his attention returned there. When I twisted around again to face Alice, she was huddled in the corner of the back seat.

"It was a store, Mom." Terra gave me one of her famous eye rolls from under cover of overhanging bangs. "What do you expect?"

I gave her a snort in return for the eye roll. "It was after hours. Besides, I can't see Mr. Worldly Jackson James as the sort of customer who would wander into an arts and craft shoppe, can you?"

"It's a gallery," Alice said, "not a craft shoppe."

"Then why don't you call it that?" Terra asked.

Alice sniffed and fumbled for a tissue in her purse. "Because it's so much more than just one thing."

Terra shrugged. "Well then, who knows why he was in there? Who knows who he really is? Just because he works in the same place where Dad..."

"Where he and your dad *worked*," I said, finishing her sentence for her.

"Nellie..." my dad warned.

My daughter cringed as if I'd just struck her. She didn't like hearing the past tense about her father anymore than I had liked it hearing about Alice's artist renter. Alice didn't seem to like it either, hearing us use the past tense to describe her arts and craft shoppe.

Excuse me, *gallery*.

I guess I couldn't blame her. It was her home, too, as well as her business, just like my situation at the karate studio. The difference being that Alice owned her building and I did not own mine.

Owner or not, it didn't matter. I wouldn't have wanted to see my place go up in smoke, either. Luckily, there had been none of our usual Boulder winds the night before to carry a flying ember across the short distance to the roof of the karate studio.

But I was getting ahead of myself. I had a way of doing that, or so Terra always reminded me.

We were still missing Felix.

We dropped Terra off at the high school, site of band camp. She handed over Sammy to Alice, who fortunately, was not unaccustomed to handling the ferret. Sammy immediately squealed and went for Alice's shiny silver, bangly earrings, sniffing them, or checking for a way to remove them to add to her collection of treasures.

My place was only a few blocks away and up the hill from the high school, so it didn't take Dad long before he pulled into the alley behind the studio. Next door, the blackened brick walls of Alice's shoppe came into view. It was hard not to notice all the extra vehicles parked around the perimeter, including a couple of cop cars. Seals on some of the car doors identified them as belonging to the fire investigation team. Cops patrolled the perimeter while suited-up guys who might be firefighters trudged in and out of the rubble that surrounded the charred shell of Alice's house.

We climbed out of the truck, I thanked Dad for the ride, and invited him in for a cup of coffee. Or a tomato juice. He mumbled something about having "too many danged errands to do," and scraped the gears into reverse. Retired life seemed to keep him busier than ever.

I turned to Alice. "What are you going to do now?" I said, trying to distract her from the activity at her ruined house. "Do you have a place to go?"

"No-where," she said with a sniff.

Movement in a bush startled me, and Sammy too, who clutched the back of Alice's neck. A pair of blue eyes watched us from the bush, and then a Siamese cat emerged from the bush and scolded us with a yelping yowl.

"Kitti Kandi!" Alice cried. She passed Sammy to me and then scooped up the cat. She hugged her tight, burying her face in fur. "Here you are! I thought we'd lost you. Poor kitty! Did Felix leave you behind? Why didn't he tell me? Even if it was only for a couple of days, he should've told me to keep an eye on you. See what nearly happened?"

My heart went out to her. "You can both stay with us as long as you need to," I said, readjusting my grip on Sammy. Her squirmy body language indicated delight at the invitation.

The cat twisted out of Alice's arms, plopped down to the gravel, and streaked across the parking area. As fast as the cat had darted, she now came to a full stop and then sauntered to the back door of the karate studio. She sat down on the step and turned to give us a scathing look that said, "Where were you all night? Don't you know there are bears and mountain lions out there?" She licked her paw. She'd already moved in.

"Really? You mean that? You don't mind Kandi, too? That's awfully kind of you."

I laughed. "Don't be so sure. I don't know how Kandi and Sammy will get along. And the accommodations aren't the best. We only have three rooms—my room, Terra's room, and the living room. But don't worry, you can have my room. It's a place to stay until you figure out what you're going to do and find something more suitable."

"No way. I'll take the couch. You're generous enough as it is. I'm not going to make you move out of your room. I promise not to get in your hair. You don't know how much this means to me. From your place, I can keep an eye on things over at..." She sniffed and nodded at the rubbled remains of her property.

"Let's start off with some iced tea, shall we?" I picked up my overnight bag and steered Alice away from the parking space off the alley. My garage-turned-shed concealed the ruins of Alice's arts and craft shoppe.

"Excuse me, ladies," said a man's voice as he hustled around the corner of the shed.

I recognized the flippant voice right away, along with his swaggering step and garishly colored sport coat. His birth certificate, I was told, had officially listed his name as James Colondoski, but we all knew him as Jimmie Condo.

I'd had a run-in or two with this developer, thwarting his plans to pave over half of Boulder with blocky, characterless concrete condominiums. Now he was sniffing around Alice's ruined house in his trademark bow tie, lime-green plaid jacket, and white trousers with a smudge of ash. Hadn't he noticed the rocketing heat? It was already in the upper eighties and the day had scarcely begun. His cat-got-the-mouse grin on his face indicated that he had bigger fish to fry than us.

"Oh, it's you," Alice said.

"Why yes, my dear, your good fortune has arrived. The papers are ready for you to sign. We have a slot open this morning at my office for just such an occasion. Shall we?" He crooked one elbow, offering it to Alice, and tipped his head in the direction of the cars, wedged into parking spaces along the alley. Wispy strands of hair fluttered from the sandy gray fringe that stood out as if electrified around a balding crown.

"I'm sorry," Alice said, not budging so much as a muscle, "I'm not ready to sell."

He folded one arm against his chest and stroked his chin. "Hmmm. Money, then, is that it? My dear, my offer is already above what your postage stamp lot is worth."

Alice nodded. "It's a generous offer."

Condo's stroking arm dropped, and he flicked his wrist, revealing an expensive gold watch. "Shall we say half past eleven, then? Can you be ready by then? I shall tell the front office to expect you." He turned and dashed toward one of the cars, a red Lexus, before either of us had a chance to breathe, let alone tell him anything contrary to his plans.

"Wow," I said. "Don't let me keep you."

"Ignore him. I need to go talk to the investigators." Alice frowned, ducking her head. She veered away from me and hurried over to the nearest officer.

I followed along, unsure if my role was to protect her, support her, or to eavesdrop on her conversation with the officials.

"Ma'am, please stay back," said the officer.

"But Officer," Alice said, "that's my house. I mean, that *was* my house." She sighed. "No, I guess it still is. It's just that I have so much work to do now. Where do I begin?" The back of her shoulders shuddered as tears overcame her once again.

"I'm sorry, ma'am. Someone will be in touch with you as part of the investigation. In the meanwhile, the experts are monitoring for hot spots and initiating their determination of cause. Where can we reach you when we're ready to talk?"

I interrupted. "She'll be staying next door with me." I pointed to the karate studio. "C'mon, Alice, let's let them do their work."

I dragged her forcefully away, listening to her sniffle behind me. The cat, waiting on the porch steps, scampered inside as I opened the door. I swear Kandi tried to trip us as we made our way through the studio and up the creaky, wooden steps to Terra's and my apartment. Alice and the cat were welcome to stay with us as long as they needed. Given the cramped quarters, I figured it wouldn't be long until Alice found another solution to her situation.

Especially if she was on the couch. Mine was a futon and barely more comfortable than Mother's.

Terra and I had had to throw together our décor with this and that. I'd rented out my house in the suburbs as a furnished home to a visiting professor, so I'd had to leave the choicer pieces behind. Here, we made do with a few cast-offs from Dad and the giveaway remains from garage sales. I'd built tables and shelves with lumber scraps from Dad's shed, and raided yards of gingham and paisleys from Mother's fabric-aholic days to cover the rustic supports.

All this gave my place a bizarre, eclectic appearance with a cozy, warm feel. It wasn't much, but to make up for the cheap edge, my second-floor windows had a view to die for. It looked like you could reach out and touch the Flatirons, Boulder's famous backdrop of rock slabs pressed against the Front Range of mountains.

Unfortunately, the view today also showed the charred brick shell of Alice's shoppe.

"Pee-you," I said, holding my nose. "How long is this smoke stink going to last?"

"Sorry." Alice lowered her chin, and I regretted my observation. Still, it was hard not to notice the smell.

"No worries. We'll have our tea outside. Let me get the windows open first, and maybe a fan going to air out the place."

A few minutes later we carried our tea outside to my back yard, where we sat at the picnic table. Having given up on a real grass lawn, I'd thrown down a plastic sheet and covered it with pea-sized gravel and pots of petunias to simulate a terrace behind the karate studio. We nursed frosty glasses of herbal iced tea and comforted ourselves with each other's presence. My friend was in trouble. Her bubbling personality had fizzled out. Alice had only been my friend for a few months, mostly since summer started, when we'd both been lured outside to our gardens. That is, *her* garden and my weed patch. But we'd hit it off, mainly over food. Just like my best friend Ruth and I, before Ruth moved away a couple of babies ago (although they were no longer babies).

Alice and I shared chemistry, just as Ruth and I had. She'd brought over a plate of chocolate chip cookies when Terra and I moved in. What better way to win one's heart than through chocolate? Cookies and gardening eventually progressed to chats over iced tea in her garden, which was a better choice—until today—than my gravel terrace. Now, only a few short months later, we were fast friends, but I really didn't know her that well. I knew she'd moved here from California, like so many other transplants to Boulder. I thought she'd fled something unpleasant back there, but she never talked about it. I knew she was into organic gardening and had dreamed of becoming a subsistence farmer if only she'd had a large enough place and a jillion other "if only's." As it was, she recycled most everything that she could find a second and third use for.

Finally, I ventured to speak, breaking the silence. "So, what movie did you see?"

"Movie?"

"You know. Last night. Before..." I didn't want to say the word "fire" and set her off again.

Her eyes darted back and forth, and she tugged at a wisp of her strawberry blonde hair, already falling down from hair pins. "Oh, I don't know. It wasn't very good. Some piece of fluff. I don't remember titles."

"What was it about?" Not that I could afford the movies very often.

"I guess it didn't grab me."

"Nothing you recommend, then?"

"Right." She sniffled and watched the cat creep up on a bee.

I watched, too, until the bee flew away. So much for Kandi's hunting skills. "What did you mean last night when you said this couldn't be happening again?"

"Did I say that?" Alice reached for her sweating glass.

"Yep."

"I have no idea." She narrowed her eyes and stared off into space—the empty space that Jimmie Condo's Lexus had left behind.

"I just thought...maybe you'd gone through this before. You know, a fire. In California. How horrible would that be?"

"Pretty much."

"So, did you?"

"Did I what?"

"Lose your house in a fire in California? Was that why you answered Mrs. Harris's ad and came to Boulder?"

"Not exactly."

I tried another angle, to get her to open up. "Do you ever think about going back to California again?"

"Oh no. Never. That's quite impossible. I couldn't possibly. That place is finished for me. As of five years, four months, and three weeks ago. Not that I'm counting."

"Okay." I didn't believe her. "Isn't that where your family is from?"

"Yes, but so was *he*. No, I can't go back where anyone could find me and dig all that up again. Besides, there's nothing for me there. But then, now there's nothing left for me here, either." Tears filled her eyes, and I reached across the table to stroke her arm.

Alarm bells rang in my mind. *He?*

"Someone is looking for you?" I said. "Someone you need protection from? Maybe you should tell me, in case he shows up here. If he can find you there, he can find you here, too." I didn't mean to worry her, but there it was.

She shook her head back and forth. Wrinkle lines streaked across her face into sort of a smile as she struggled, gulping back tears. "No-o-o-o! It's too late for that."

"It's okay, honey. Go ahead and cry. Let it out."

"That's all I did last night. I'm all cried out." She sniffed, and then gave out a feeble laugh. "Really, I am. It's just that, I thought I was safe here. In Boulder, I mean. Now I'm not so sure."

"You think he's found you here?"

Her head wagged some more, and then bobbed up and down. Apparently, she couldn't make up her mind what she thought. "It's p-payback," she finally blurted out.

"Then, you think...this person...set the fire? Trying to hurt you?"

More head bobbling. "N-no. Oh, Nell, I don't know what to think." Another sniff. "Someone has. Look, I don't want to drag you into this...this *mess*. Maybe I should go away." She started to rise from the table.

I pressed her hand down to the wooden surface. "You'll do no such thing. But I can't help you if I don't know what we're up against."

"I...that is, he..." She sank down to her seat and bit her lower lip. "I don't know where to start. You see, I had this boyfriend. He never meant to hurt me, really he didn't. He just hated the way I spent so much time blowing glass. It was my creative release, but I had to go to a studio to do it. I thought he'd like the extra income from what I sold. It was mostly commission work. But no, I couldn't ever seem to do anything right to make him happy—"

"Okay, I get the picture."

"No. You don't—"

"Honey, there's no excuse for hurting someone. It's not up to you to make him happy to keep him from hurting you. You did the right thing, walking away."

"I guess...you're right. I'm not going back."

"Of course you're not. You're staying right here. You can start again, once you get the insurance money."

"Do you know how hard it is to start over?"

Oh boy, did I.

I ducked my head so that she wouldn't see the fire that still simmered in my soul. My husband, Max, had put it there when he, the weasel, backed out of his vows and abandoned Terra and me. And stuck me with all the bills.

"We'll be your family," I said once I doused my inner flames. "You can build again. I'll help you get started."

"I dunno." She sighed. "It'd be easier to let someone else do the building. Maybe I should accept that Condo fellow's offer."

"Don't do anything hasty. I don't trust him. He wanted to buy this place, too. My boss told him to go away."

"What was he planning to do? Build more student housing?"

"I think he's more interested in putting a senior citizen home here."

"Here? This close to the university?"

"Seniors have more money."

"Everyone wants to make a fast buck, don't they?"

I couldn't argue with that. Somehow, we had to make a living. There was always the option of going back home to live with my dad. Let him support Terra and me. He'd love it, in fact. But no way. That would be the same as defeat. Admitting that I couldn't make it on my own in the adult world.

It wasn't much, what I had here, but it was my gig.

"At least now, with the insurance," Alice said with a sigh, "I'll actually have money coming *into* my account instead of going out."

"I gather your craft shoppe wasn't making you tons of money?" I glanced at the blackened ruins on the other side of the shrubs.

Alice snorted. Tea splashed up her nose. "First off, it's a *gallery*, not a 'craft shoppe.' We display and sell locally made items of arts and crafts. Nothing fancy like the galleries downtown. Think of us more as a year-round bazaar. And no, there's not a lot of money in quilted hotpads."

"We? Us?" Who else was she talking about? Jackson James? Why else would he have been caught in the fire in her store?

Alice sighed with the sound of regret of having lost a lot more than her livelihood. "A figure of speech. I wouldn't be in business without the various artists who want to display their work in my shoppe." She sighed deeper. "Now they've lost their work, too. It's not just me and my house. They've lost irreplaceable, one-of-a-kind creations."

"They're not going to blame you. The fire wasn't your fault."

She smiled wryly. "Wasn't it? I mean, not that it was. But what if it's payback for my past? You see, I *am* responsible. Anyway, there will be the doubters. There will be those who will think it was me who actually started that fire to collect the insurance money." Her arms sprawled across the top of the picnic table, and she laid her head down between them and sobbed. "I'm going to have to settle up with each one of them about their losses."

"Can't you let your insurance company do that?"

"Of course, they will when it comes time to pay out. In the meanwhile, I'll have to check computer records to find out which of their items hadn't sold. I had some paper records filed in fireproof boxes. I wonder if those boxes really do what they're supposed to do? I guess we'll find out. Thank goodness everything got backed up into the cloud. That's what Robinette mainly does for me, all the computer stuff. But I'll still need to confirm with each of the artists to establish what pieces hadn't sold. If they were destroyed by fire, smoke, or water, then insurance will pay for them. I just don't think I have the strength to face all the artists now. And until I get something from insurance, I can't afford to pay Robinette to do it."

"What if I helped you with that?"

"I can't pay you, either, at least not right away."

"Who said anything about paying me?"

"Oh, Nell, you're too kind. You've already done so much for me."

"It's not that much. After Terra gets home from band camp today, she can help with the computer stuff and create a list of names and addresses for me with an inventory of their unsold pieces. Tomorrow morning I can start contacting those people."

Her voice wavered. "Some of them are going to tell you that my shoppe has become more profitable writing it off to insurance than it ever was doing business."

"Don't worry. They'll cooperate if they want to be reimbursed for their losses."

She moaned and lowered her head again. "It's too much. How will I ever repay you?"

"You don't have to. It's what friends are for."

"But I insist." She lifted up, brightening. "Wait a minute. I have an idea. Maybe I could paint a picture for you." She glanced up at the second floor windows of the karate studio, as if she could see through them, to my bare walls.

"You paint, too, as well as blowing glass?"

She blushed. "I used to. I've been meaning to take it up again. I was hoping Felix would inspire me."

"Then, you should go for it. I'd love to have an original by you."

We both fell silent, weighted down by the heaviness of events. Would painting restore joy to Alice's soul or weight her down even further with a self-imposed obligation? My gaze drifted across the shrubs to the bright yellow tape surrounding her blackened brick walls next door. Even outside, there was still a taste of smoke in the air. But inside, the smell was far worse. It would make breathing too difficult while working out. I would have to cancel formal classes today.

The sound of hammering broke into our silence. We looked at each other, then scanned the landscape for the sound. It wasn't coming from the charred ruins next door. Someone was pounding on my front door. Then a man's voice accompanied the knocking.

"Police. Open up!"

Four

THE POLICE HAD *finally caught me.*

That was my immediate reaction to the sound of the officer's voice. Along with a splinter scrape as I jerked against the picnic table.

Not that I was guilty of anything.

Fears weren't rational.

Breathe, Nell.

Maybe I wasn't being so irrational. At least one officer on the force—Detective Rosenquist—had made his suspicions of me clear enough these last nine months, since my husband Max went missing. Last November, Max left the house to teach his class at the university, but he never showed up there. He'd been AWOL ever since.

At first, we all feared the worst. But as the weeks dragged on, with still no evidence of Max, Rosenquist became my personal nemesis. He was certain I was the unsavory reason behind the mystery of my husband's whereabouts. And maybe I was. Because later, we heard second-hand reports that Max had simply checked out of his strait-laced, stress-inducing lifestyle (had I stressed him?) for a more relaxed one in the Caribbean with a longhaired honey—*and* with funds from our joint savings account. But none of those reports had stopped Rosenquist from pestering me with his suspicions.

What now?

Junipers and police tape from next door clogged the side yard, so I ran inside through the back door and hurried through the studio. Alice charged close to my heels. I pulled open the front door to reveal not Rosenquist standing on the front porch but his rookie partner instead, Sean Hennesey. A detective, he dressed in casual slacks and a tan polo shirt.

Were these the only two cops in the entire police department? Or did they take an extra special interest in my neighborhood?

"Well, hello again," I said lamely.

"Ma'am." Detective Hennesey dipped his chin, and a chunk of his bushy hair, the color and texture of straw, flopped forward.

"Where's your partner?" I said.

"Reassigned, ma'am."

I scanned the street behind Hennesey. Usually, with Rosenquist in tow, their unmarked vehicle parked in the middle of the street as their solution to the parking problem, meaning the lack thereof. Today I didn't see any sedan blocking traffic.

"What's wrong? What's happened?"

"I'm looking for Alice Albright." Hennesey's impassive gaze focused on a spot behind my shoulder.

"Yes, Officer, that's me." She stepped out from behind me. "What can I do for you? Have you found the cause of the fire yet?"

"They're still working on it, ma'am."

"Wait a minute," I said, frowning at Hennesey. "What are *you* doing here? Did you get reassigned, too? Are you working fire investigation now, instead of homicide?"

"No, ma'am, special assignment." Hennesey stepped around me, staring straight at Alice. "If you don't mind, ma'am, would you come along with me? We only have a few questions for you."

"Questions? Why are you asking *me*? Do I need a lawyer?"

"Just a minute," I said. "What about her rights? She doesn't have to talk to you."

"That's true," Hennesey said, rubbing his clean-shaven jaw, "but I was hoping she'd cooperate, and we could get to the bottom of this."

"The bottom of what? Am I under arrest?"

"No, ma'am, we just want to talk to you."

"What do you want to talk to her about?" I said. "She can't tell you anything. She wasn't even home when the fire broke out."

Hennesey's jaw tightened as he glanced from Alice to me, the nuisance, and back to Alice again. "This isn't the best place to talk, out here on your front porch."

"You can talk inside," I said, my heart pattering erratically. It wasn't *that* smoky inside, was it? "You don't have to take her to headquarters." I remembered the last time I was there and how traumatized the experience had left me. Granted, that had been under Rosenquist's hostile questioning methods and not his nicer, easier-going partner.

"I don't mind." Alice breezed past me, leaving behind a whiff of the strawberry shower gel I kept at Dad's. "You know this officer, Nell. Of course I'll cooperate."

I watched her climb into the passenger's side of his unmarked sedan parked legally in front of the studio. At least it wasn't the rear seat of a cop car for criminals. Hennesey strode around to the driver's side, made a motion to me with his fingers, tapping the side of his head in some sort of farewell salute, climbed in and drove away, past the ruins of Alice's house.

Sheesh, would I ever see Alice again?

I breathed some more. I had to think about all this.

For me, there was no better way to think than on a morning run. I needed my daily conditioning, anyway, and the inside of the studio was too smoky for a good workout. Alice was away, otherwise occupied, so what else could I do?

I sprinted upstairs, checked on Sammy who curled asleep in her hammock in her ferret condo, and changed into my running gear. The ASPCA would probably arrest me for leaving her behind in a smoky environment. Ten minutes later, I tied my house key to my shoelaces and set out.

Left or right?

I flipped a mental coin and chose left, the direction that would take me to Broadway, the major street that bordered the university.

I liked running in the morning before the world fully woke up, before the angst of the day set in. In truth, it wasn't that early, but the academics moved in a morning fog. And I already had plenty of angst.

Were they going to blame my new best friend for burning down her own house?

Nell, Nell, came Master Hwang's voice in my head.

I know, I know. I had to get rid of my negative thinking. My master sensei had only told me a thousand times, not counting all the mental reminders.

Call me suspicious, but I couldn't help but wonder if Alice's fire had something to do with money. Apparently her finances were a wreck, and Felix hadn't helped matters by missing his rent payments. Or was the fire the result of revenge from a rejected boyfriend in California?

I crossed Broadway at the traffic light and glided onto a path at the perimeter of the tree-lined campus. Passersby shuffled in a quiet daze before their morning lattes kicked in. The university, only a few blocks away from my apartment, was my private park at this hour with its centurion trees and massive, sandstone buildings housing lecture halls. They looked to me like something I called "western Victorian." They weren't. In architecture talk, they were something else, Italian something-or-other.

I wondered if Alice's shaky finances had started that crazy neighbor's gossip the night before.

Next, Alice would be accused of setting the fire to get the insurance money. Were the police going to arrest her for *that*?

I had to do something. I couldn't stand by and see that happen. My feet pounded harder. My breathing grew shallow and erratic.

The old part of campus transitioned to a newer section, where massive replicas of the original western Victorians dwarfed the landscape, each one bigger than the next, owing to the stature of its faculty and grant money. Old or new, sandstone and red tile roofs pulled the grounds of the campus together.

How could I help Alice?

My thoughts kept spinning as I circled the borders of the campus. Poor Alice. She would be devastated. Losing a house was bad enough. Losing her business, and being blamed for it, was even worse. And on top of that, she was already dealing with whatever had gone down in California. An ex-boyfriend.

My ex had worked in one of these buildings that I was huffing and puffing past. Technically, Max wasn't "ex" yet, but he soon would be, as soon as the paperwork went through. His absence kept him from refuting any of it. I wasn't holding my breath for child support.

There must be some way I could help Alice. After all, since becoming a martial arts instructor, I'd gained some experience solving problems for my students. And I knew something about being blamed for matters outside of my control. I was as certain of Alice's innocence as I had been certain of my own. Surely I could use my own experience to help my neighbor and best friend. Alice was the first real friend I'd had in years. I couldn't stand idly by and listen to threats from an obnoxious neighbor or wait for the mysterious abusive boyfriend to arrive from California, seeking revenge against Alice for running away.

My nose throbbed where it had been punched, as a sort of reminder of my investment in Alice.

Okay. I was going to do it. Somehow. I was going to free Alice from suspicion. That meant I had to find out who did set that fire. Because it had been arson. I would bet on it.

* * * * *

Crossing Broadway again, I left the university behind and looped around through the neighborhoods. I coasted back through the alley behind the karate studio, breathing deeply, cooling off from my run. The pitcher of iced tea and our glasses, warmed now from the late summer sun, still sat on the picnic table where Alice and I had left them. Seeing the reminders of our companionship made me all the more determined to help my friend.

I stretched my running muscles as I propped myself against the table and then poured a fresh glass. Even though the ice cubes had melted in the pitcher, it was liquid and still refreshing. I had to force myself not to guzzle it down too fast.

Scraping, swishing sounds alerted me to something in the bushes. Branches waved, rattling the old, gnarled lilac bush growing between my weed patch and Alice's back door. I spied a man over there, in a Hawaiian shirt and Panama hat, bending over the singed grass behind Alice's house. He didn't look much like a fire investigator. He scuffed through some rubble as if looking for something, then circled around the bush. When he came into view, straightened, and caught sight of me, we recognized each other right away.

"Hello, Jack." I managed to find my voice. Jackson James! What on earth was he doing *here*?

"Eleanor!" Jackson said, calling me by my given name, as Max had done. No wonder. They'd been colleagues at the university. He would know me as Max had.

I wondered what other details Max had gotten wrong about me and had conveyed incorrectly to his colleagues? Jackson James was everything Max had wanted to be, right down to the silvery threads of his thick hair, turning prematurely gray and poking out from beneath the brim of his white hat. Max had a hat like that, too. Max had always tried to emulate Jackson, for reasons I never understood.

Still, it was a relief to see Jackson upright after his terrible ordeal the night before.

Jackson held out his arms in greeting and trotted out from behind the lilac bush. "What a delightful surprise! I hoped I would find you here."

59

We hugged, and I frowned, puzzled. "Me?" I stepped back and searched his face. "You were looking for me? How did you know I'd be here?" I hadn't exactly been in communication with the former colleague of the husband I hadn't seen in nine months.

He waved my questions aside. "Someone must've mentioned it. Someone from the university, no doubt."

I frowned deeper. We didn't have anyone in common anymore. Unless he meant Gillian, Max's half-sister, who had used her connections and her trust fund to get accepted into graduate school here. I relaxed. That made sense. Gillian—Jill to me—had never liked my moving to the university neighborhood, corrupting her niece with these dubious surroundings. She would've talked to Jackson, trying to persuade him to talk some sense into me.

He peered closely at me, specifically at the bruise that mottled the side of my nose, threatening a black eye. "What's wrong with your face?"

"It's nothing." I stepped back, away from his scrutiny. "Just a wayward fist. But enough about me. What about *you*? How are you? Did you escape from the hospital, or did they let you go?"

"It was a rather costly detour, but I'll live."

He didn't seem any worse for wear after a night in the hospital for smoke inhalation, but he hadn't answered my question. "But how are your lungs? You were very lucky."

"You heard about all that?"

"Of course. I live here. What were you doing in Alice's store last night, anyway, after it had closed for the day?"

He shoved his fists into his jeans pockets and moved some

pebbles around with the toes of his tennis shoes. "I, uh, was visiting my, uh, girlfriend."

"You have a *girl*friend?" I had always thought he was gay, after Gillian's embarrassing fiasco with him shortly after she'd moved to town. I'd even entertained some doubts on occasion about him and Max—doubts that had been put to rest when I'd found long black hairs on Max's blazer.

Jackson nodded, and color flushed up his neck and face.

"And you were visiting her in the store?"

Good grief.

Was he talking about *Alice*? Surely not Robinette, not with their age difference. But Alice... Yeah, maybe. Alice claimed she had gone to the movies last night, but she could've really been out with Jackson on a date. Although, why keep their relationship a secret? I rejected the thought almost as fast as it came to me. I would've known, if my friend was seeing someone. And anyway, Jackson had been inside the burning house while Alice was already away.

I didn't know what to say to my suspicions, so I laughed and changed the subject. "I just can't believe they'd let you out of the hospital this soon, and then you would come straight back here."

He laughed too, but it didn't sound convincing. "Where would you have me go? The fire is out, and I wanted to see the remains for myself. Have you seen inside this place?"

"No, they won't let anyone in there. Jackson, you didn't go *inside*, did you?"

He shrugged.

"You can't go in there. You want something to collapse on you and send you back to the hospital?"

"You know if he's all right? I couldn't go anywhere before I found out."

"Felix, you mean? The artist?" I frowned. "Alice thought maybe he'd gone out of town to paint outdoors for a few days."

"You mean...he's okay?" Jackson tugged on his shirt collar and broke into a coughing fit.

"As far as I know. Good thing he missed this. Look, how about something to drink? I have iced tea, although the ice has melted by now."

He nodded and bent over from his waist as his chest spasmed with wracking coughs. I steered him to the picnic table, sat him down, and ran into the back office of the studio where I kept a supply of paper cups. Within a few minutes, his coughing had passed, and he was sipping his tea.

"Are you sure you're okay?"

"I'll be fine." He wiped the tears from the corners of his eyes. I couldn't tell if his tears were from his coughing fit or from relief that Felix was safe.

He inhaled deeply and gave me a twisted smile. "Then, I guess my timing wasn't so lucky after all. No sooner had I pulled into my parking spot last night than...er, a young lady came running outside, crying and calling for help. She said someone was trapped inside. I assumed it was Felix. Do you know his work? Amazing. Just amazing. His mountain landscapes are the best." Jackson lowered his head over his cup of tea. His hands shook as he brought the cup up to his mouth and drank.

"That would've been Robinette," I said. "She came here, too, super hysterical. She must've been mistaken. I had no idea she'd already found some help. You, Jack."

"I ran in to help him, but... I couldn't."

I touched his arm. "It was good of you to try to help."

"I couldn't breathe, and..." His trembling fingers knocked his cup over. He took a deep breath. "I couldn't find him."

"Because he wasn't there. Robinette didn't know he was away."

"Maybe not, but she said loud and clear, 'he's upstairs,' but I... The smoke was too thick. I couldn't get up there. And the next thing I knew, someone was carrying me outside." He shuddered with sighs.

"You were very lucky."

He sighed again and looked over his shoulder. "I've been wanting to know about Felix ever since, but no one would tell me anything. Besides, I had to take a taxi over here, since this is where I'd left my car."

"A taxi, really? Your girlfriend couldn't give you a ride?" I wanted to know more about her. Maybe she lived in one of these houses nearby. Or in the apartment building across the alley. Mostly students lived there. Was Jackson dating a *student*?

"She doesn't have a car. Besides, I wanted to talk to you."

"Me? What about?"

"My dear, I'm done here. They canned me. Oh, not quite yet. They can't, not with tenure and all, but we've reached an accord, and I won't be coming back for the fall term. I have another position lined up in Denver, but I don't plan to leave Boulder completely. I still have my mountain home up the canyon. You remember it? We had a division picnic there once."

I nodded. I remembered. Max had made a fool of himself, flirting with one of the school secretaries who wasn't at all interested in him. His flirting turned into harassment. "I'm sorry to hear about your job. It's going to be a terrible commute in the winter."

"Not really, since I only use my home on weekends any more. I leased a small apartment in Denver a couple months ago. I will probably have to sell the mountain home, though, unless I can come up with some quick cash. You wouldn't happen to know of any good money-making ventures?"

"If I did, I wouldn't be here, teaching martial arts."

He surveyed the karate studio and frowned. "You are a woman of many talents, my dear."

"I do my best."

Something about this conversation felt off to me. Why was Jackson surfacing *now* in my life? "What did you want to talk to me about?" Surely, not to tell me about his move. "Has something come up? Have you heard from Max?"

He shook his head a little too emphatically. I wasn't sure I believed him.

"I worry about you, Eleanor. That was a shitty thing for Max to do, pardon my French, the way he left you high and dry like that."

I nodded, but I still didn't believe him. There was something more... Something left unsaid... A subtle warning about Max, perhaps, a warning to be prepared for another possible encounter. "Thanks, Jackson, it's kind of you to worry about me. Don't worry. I'm doing okay."

He leaned closer. "I feel responsible for you, in a way. I want to make it up to you. Perhaps you'd like to use my mountain place sometime, as a little getaway?"

"That's very generous of you, but there's no need to feel responsible for me. Besides, it's hard for me to get away now. I teach six days per week."

"Oh, then you must arrange it for your seventh day. All you have to remember is the code into the garage: High."

"Hi?"

"H-i-g-h, as in... Well, you know."

I smiled. "Thanks, I'll keep it in mind, but really, I'm doing fine. Don't worry about me." Actually, I was doing *great,* now that I'd landed my own two feet.

"Well, you see, I'm afraid I'm the one who lured Max away from your hearth. He wanted to take that cooking class with me at LePuc's, remember?"

How could I not?

"We made the most fantastic soufflés, by the way. Who would've thought, at this altitude?"

"Right." I sniffed, regretting all the losses of what had never been. "It wasn't your fault. Max made his own decisions about what he did in his spare time." I tried to smile. "Are you still cooking?"

"Me? Hell, no. I'm in to painting these days. If only I had a fraction of Felix's talent..." He stared at the blackened chimney creeping up the side of Alice's wall. "That's how I met Felix, at cooking school. It was through that young lady who works in his studio—Robinette, I think is her name? She worked the reception desk part-time at LePuc's, and she brought in information about Felix's paint class. So I thought 'why not'?"

My mind spun, trying to process the circuitry of these connections. "So, Robinette was doing Felix a favor by recruiting students for him?"

"That's one way to look at it. She thinks the world of him, you know. We all do." He looked over his shoulder again and lowered his voice. "I don't suppose anyone has come around here looking for him? Asking questions? Maybe about a fireproof box?"

"The investigators. Is that who you mean? And the police. Do they count?"

"No, no, not the police. I'm talking about any suspicious-looking characters lurking around."

"Alice said she kept papers in a fireproof box, but why would anyone want them?"

"Not papers. Money, what else? That's where Felix keeps his cash. I think someone is after it, and now they're after me."

I made a mental note to ask Alice if she knew about Felix's fireproof box of money. If he had cash set aside, then he should've used it to pay Alice the rent money he owed her.

"Why in the world would they be after *you*?" I asked. Jackson was always the paranoid type.

"Because they think I was there last night to take it. That maybe I hid it."

"But who wants Felix's money?" Other than Alice, that is.

"Tell you what. If you see anyone suspicious around here, looking as if they're looking for something, you call me right away, okay?" He pulled a business card from his pocket and pushed it into my hand.

"Sure, Jack."

"Oh no, now what?" A deadened look glazed his eyes as he stared vacantly past my head.

I turned and looked. Through the bushes I saw movement next door. Uniformed people strode briskly around an ambulance parked in front of Alice's house. It must've driven up without a siren. I moved up onto the back porch, where I got a better view above the bushes. The rear doors of the ambulance angled open, and a paramedic waited nearby with a gurney. Two fire investigators in heavy-duty boots and bulky lime green coveralls tromped down the sidewalk, carrying out a bulky body bag between them. They placed it on the gurney and helped the paramedic shove it all into the rear door of the waiting ambulance.

Omigod. They'd found a body in Alice's burned house.

Felix.

Was it *Felix*?

It had to be Felix, the missing artist. He hadn't been away painting after all, not as Alice thought.

I was vaguely aware of Jackson at my side. There was a yelp—his or mine? Next thing I knew, he'd jumped down from the porch and sprinted away, toward a line of cars parked in the alley.

Dread washed over me as I realized Hennesey must've already known about this. That's why a homicide cop was taking Alice to headquarters to talk to her. It wouldn't look good for Alice's case if she had a lower opinion of Felix than the rest of the world. Jackson had made it sound as if everyone thought Felix walked on water.

And now he was dead. Murdered? This wasn't just about a fire anymore.

It was murder by fire.

Five

A SILVER CAR ROARED to life in the alley and spewed gravel as it shot away. I didn't know why Jackson was in such a hurry. One thing felt certain. He'd been lying to me about something.

I plunged into the karate studio, through the back door, and raced out the front. I darted off the porch and ran up the hill toward the ambulance, almost as fast as Jackson's car had abandoned me. "Excuse me!"

The investigators had already turned back toward Alice's burned house, and the paramedic focused on his process of latching the rear door shut. I shouted louder. One of the investigators stopped and looked up as the paramedic climbed into the ambulance and drove away. No sirens, no flashing lights. It was too late for any of that.

"Was that a body you just now brought out?" I asked the investigators. Silent, they watched me charge toward them. Just because it was a body *bag*, I thought, didn't necessarily mean that a body had been *inside* it.

The investigators exchanged a glance between themselves, then their gazes drifted down the hill to the karate studio next door, where I had emerged. Was that a smirk on their faces? They had written me off as a nosy neighbor.

Well, maybe I was.

So what?

"I'm sorry, ma'am," one of them said, definitely fighting a smirk. "We aren't privileged to give out information at the moment."

I huffed a sigh of exasperation. "Look. Help me out here. I'm worried about the status of my neighbor, you see. He's an artist by the name of Felix Todd. No one seems to know where he is. And anyway, I'm not just being nosy. Really. I'm not asking about him for *my* sake. I'm asking for my friend, the owner of this house that burned. You see, she's staying with me for now, since she's out of a home, except she's gone to the police station, I guess to make a statement about all this. Except she doesn't know about this. Are they going to tell her about this poor victim they found inside her house, or should I? What am I going to tell her?"

"The professionals will handle it, ma'am, thanks for asking." The fire investigators turned and clomped back toward the charred house.

"It *is* Felix, isn't it?" I shouted at their backs, but they disappeared through the remains of the front door. "I know it is!"

Well, heck. They weren't going to talk to me.

* * * * *

I stewed some more and then phoned Jimmie Condo's office. His receptionist, who had papers ready for Alice to sign, hadn't seen Alice, either.

Over the lunch hour, I would normally do a round of

strengthening and conditioning exercises before the first class of the day, but today was hardly normal. I couldn't get Jackson's bizarre behavior out of my mind. He'd taken off in a state of agitation, almost as if he'd been afraid of something. So much for any concern about Felix.

I kept puzzling about LePuc's, too. After all, Jackson had brought it up. It was the cooking school that Max had attended with Jackson—and now I'd learned that Felix had been there, too. The coincidence of it all didn't bode well in my bones. I would have to check it out.

LePuc's School of the Culinary Arts hid behind a nondescript glass and metal door in a small shopping strip on the east side of town. There was a nail salon on one side of the school and an organic pet food store on the other. I thought about picking up treats for Sammy and Kandi, except they'd probably reject anything too healthy.

A text beeped on my phone as I parked the Ghia in a spacious lot.

Gillian: *Meet for lunch?*

Me: *Sure. Where?*

Gillian: *Greens.*

I sighed. *Greens* was my soon-to-be-ex sister-in-law's new favorite salad bar on the pedestrian mall downtown. Which meant a battle for parking, especially now, in summer tourist season (not to be confused with winter tourist season). Boulder would ban cars altogether, if it could.

Me: *See u there in 30.*

Grinning at my tech savviness, I turned off my phone altogether. Mainly, it was to unchain myself from Max's half-sister, who was accustomed to controlling everyone and

71

everything around her.

When I stepped out onto the blazing pavement, warmth seeped through the soles of my sandals, and I stepped swiftly across the parking lot toward LePuc's single door. Butcher-block paper was taped to the inside of the glass windows and door of the cooking school preventing passersby from accidentally stealing their culinary secrets. I tugged on the door—it was locked—but someone from inside buzzed me in. Glancing up, I spied the white box of a security camera aimed down at me. I pulled the door open, and air conditioning swept over me, caressing my face. A savory smell of garlic made my stomach rumble.

A woman's voice sang greeting pleasantries to me from behind a reception counter. "Good afternoon! You're here to sign up for a class? Please start by filling out a registration form, so that we can reserve a space for you. Classes are filling fast!"

I stepped to the chest-high counter and peered over its top, hoping to find Robinette. Instead, Ms. Sunshine grinned up at me. A tiny thing, she appeared even smaller than my own superlightweight frame. That would make her shorter than my five feet, and less than my one hundred pounds.

"I'm not here for a class," I said.

"Oh." Her smile evaporated, and she reached for the receiver of her sleek desk phone.

"I'm looking for information."

She dropped the phone back into its cradle. "I don't have much of that to give you. I'm pretty good at taking credit cards, though."

I made up my story on the spot. "Some friends of mine took a class together a while back and recommended it. I was hoping to find out when that class would be offered again, so that I can take it, too."

"What was the class?"

"See, that's the thing," I said, hoping my giggle didn't sound too fake. "I can't remember exactly. It was something about 'making the impossible soufflé possible.' Max and Jackson were only interested in gourmet cooking."

"Max, did you say?" Frowning, she fingered a lock of her blonde hair and chewed on it.

"That's right. Max Gannon. Do you know him?"

She shrugged. "You should talk to the chef. Dominic LePuc."

My mind did backward flips in my head. "Dominic...?" Alice had said that Felix only allowed one person upstairs to his attic, a friend named Dominic. With a name like that, I wondered if this could be the same person.

"That's right. He's not in, though. Come back later this afternoon. He'll be in around four, prepping."

I gave her my business card and confirmed a time.

Her eyes widened as she read the card and glanced up at me, apparently trying to reconcile my title "Head Instructor" with my diminutive stature and middle-aged mom looks.

"Don't forget to like us on our FaceBook page," she said hopefully on my way out.

In your dreams.

* * * * *

The beauty of the Ghia was that it could fit in less than a full parking space. So it only took me about ten minutes to find a place to park on the edge of downtown. I hustled to meet

Gillian and found her waiting for me at a table outside on the pedestrian mall.

Gillian swirled a glass of sangría, manipulating the orange chunks and ice cubes to swirl and clink in red wine. "You turned off your phone again."

I sank down into the wrought iron chair next to hers and draped my bag—a book bag from an out-of-business mystery bookstore that I used as a catchall—across the armrest. "Nice to see you, too."

"Oh, Nell, don't be so obtuse. *Now* do you believe me?"

"About what?"

"About living in *that place*. I tried to warn you, but you wouldn't listen. Look what's happened now. You barely escaped with your lives intact. If you won't listen to me, then for God's sake, think of my niece. What kind of example are you setting for her in *that place*?"

That place was the karate studio. According to Gillian, proper young ladies wouldn't be caught dead, kicking and punching. I'd heard her complaints enough. And I ignored them.

"I guess you saw the story in the newspaper, then?"

"*And* the photos. Kind of hard to miss on the front page. And there you were, right in the middle of it. Everyone at the business school has been talking about it all morning."

"Not because of me, surely. It was probably on account of Jackson James being injured in the fire. He teaches at the B-school."

"Taught, you mean. And you don't have to tell me about Professor James."

"Right." When Gillian started her graduate studies here two

years ago, she'd lusted after the debonair professor, but her lust died quickly when snickers started surfacing about "Jack and Jill." Some might call my half-sister-in-law vain and hormone-driven, but when it came to her career path, she knew exactly what she wanted: to become the female CEO of a large company back east. Pity her poor underlings. I had never known her to fail at getting what she wanted.

It was always best to be on her side in any battle. Which was why I decided to fill her in on the case of murder by fire. And while I was at it, I let her know that Terra, Alice, and I sure could use a smoke-free place to stay temporarily.

"Of course you shall stay with me," Gillian said in her breathless, Smith-educated voice. "Why didn't you come last night?"

"We were at my dad's," I explained. "But your place is a lot more—"

"Comfortable? Of course it is."

"Convenient. Terra has band camp going on now, you see, and she can come and go on her own, if we stay in town." I suppressed a shiver of irritation and bit my tongue. After all, Jill didn't have to put us up. It was very gracious of her to offer to do so, even if she thought I was raising my daughter all wrong.

"I've been busy, too," Gillian said, switching her attention from me to her menu. "But of course you didn't get my voicemail, so never mind."

I gave up. I reached into my bag and fumbled past my car keys and wallet. Things got lost because my bag was large enough to carry other necessities, like my practice chuks. I never knew when I could grab a little extra practice at nunchaku for our upcoming demo. Luckily, they weren't the real kind—wooden flails—but fashioned instead out of lightweight rubber.

I pulled out my phone, and turned it on. Dialing up voicemail, I listened to the first of Gillian's breathless messages. She was babbling something about an investment.

But something else caught my eye. Resting underneath the clutter at the bottom of my bag was something shiny I didn't recognize. I pulled it out for a closer view.

"What's that?" Gillian said.

"I dunno. How'd this get into my bag?"

It was a piece of foil, about the size of my thumb. It looked like a label that had pulled off of a package. Perhaps it had fallen off of something I'd bought. Except... *Creations by Erica*, it read. I didn't remember making any purchase in a place called that. Under the name, it listed a website, a phone number, and a street address.

"Let me see." Gillian wiggled her fingers, and I forked it over. "It's a label that's come off of something you must have bought. The address is from your new neighborhood. *That place*, you know."

"But I didn't..." Then I remembered Samurai Q. Ferret. She had a habit of stealing shiny things. She had been absent for a while at Dad's that morning while Alice was in the shower. Eventually Sammy had turned up in Alice's room. The ferret must've stolen it from Alice's purse and squirreled it away in my bag. What a rascally, little thief!

But then I wondered why Alice would've kept this label in her purse to be stolen by a ferret, unless it had come off of something she'd bought. Or, more likely, it was contact information for one of her suppliers for the shoppe.

"Anyway, as I said in my message," Gillian said with a wave

at the phone I'd laid down beside my napkin-wrapped utensils, "no one seems to know where he is."

"Who?"

"Your artist friend, Felix Todd."

"He's not my friend."

"Okay, whatever."

"And he's dead."

"Whaaat? How do you know that?"

"Because I saw a body bag being carried out of Alice's house. It's him. I know it is, even though they wouldn't confirm it."

"Then, that explains why his paintings are being snapped up like hotcakes," Gillian said with a frown. "He exhibits regularly at Glowworm, which is a gallery downtown, in case you didn't know, since you move in, shall we say, somewhat different circles? Anyway, it's a world class gallery, and to exhibit there, his work does not come cheap. I have a call in to the family back east to see if they want to invest in one of his western landscapes. So after lunch, let's just pop over there and take a look."

"Do you even know what his style is like?"

"Doesn't matter. It's an investment. Besides, I saw samples on the internet. It's okay. The point is, his work isn't going to be available much longer, and its value is only going to skyrocket. On account of his fame, and now this."

"I hope the family likes it, if you plan to buy something for them."

"They won't. They'll store it until it becomes profitable to resell." She looked around for the server and waved her menu in the air. "Service is slow today. Must be the heat."

"They're just busy. Every table is filled."

Gillian grinned. "I got the best table, wouldn't you agree?"

"It is a nice umbrella. And we're lucky to have one on a sunny day like this."

"No, silly. We have the best view of what's happening on the mall. Notice, for instance, the man leaning against that tub of geraniums."

Without turning her head, her jade gaze swept across the paving stones beyond our patio seating area. I squinted against the glaring sun in the direction she indicated.

"No! Don't stare at him." She kicked me under the table.

"He seems to be watching the contortionist act on the mall," I said.

"He isn't," she hissed. "He's watching us."

I looked again. Khaki shorts showed off his legs as he leaned against the planter. One hairy leg angled across his other knee. A canvas fedora shaded his face.

Gillian kicked me again. "What are you going to have? You must be parched."

I turned away from the mystery man by the planter, and we gave our orders to the server. Herbal iced tea for me and salads for both of us. When the server went away, I glanced back at the planter, but the guy in the fedora was gone.

"You know who he is?" Gillian asked.

I shook my head. "Never seen him before."

Gillian tapped her plum pink fingernail against her matching lips. "He looks vaguely familiar. I've seen that chiseled profile somewhere before. It'll come to me." She took another sip of her sangría.

"I'm sure it will."

* * * * *

An empty space dominated the first display wall at Glowworm. That's where the painting had hung. It was a rectangular area, about two feet by three feet, of bare wall, painted off-white and displaying smudge marks where picture frames had rubbed against the wall. The card describing the missing painting still attached to the wall:

"Mountain High"
24x30 oil on linen
Felix Todd
$9,995

Gillian yelped. "We're too late! Who's the creep that stole it out from under us?"

I yelped at the price tag. At those prices, it was hard to believe Felix didn't have any spare cash with which to pay his rent money to Alice.

I marched past an array of paintings to the sales counter at the back of the gallery. A blonde woman with her hair pulled back in a severe bun studied her computer screen through horn-rimmed glasses that perched on the end of her sharp nose.

"Excuse me," I said. "Can you tell me about the Felix Todd painting that was on display up there?" I pointed toward the front of the gallery. Gillian had wandered off, examining other paintings.

"That one has been sold," the woman said, peering up at me over the top of her glasses. "It was our last Todd, sadly. But we have other mountain landscapes I could show you."

"No thanks. I'm only interested in his paintings. Can you tell me who bought this one?"

"A private collector. He was quite taken with it, as I recall. I doubt that he would be interested in selling it so soon."

I swiped my hand through the tangles of my hair in frustration, mussing it all the more.

"Todd's paintings have been moving fast," the woman said. "It's a pity about his fire. Art is so temporal. We've had his inventory for months, without moving a single item, and now they're all gone."

"There must be more somewhere."

"I believe everything else has burned in that fire."

"What about other galleries?"

She shook her head. "He does not display anywhere else, except on rare occasions. I'll check online, if you'd like, and see if I can find anything else."

"Please."

I waited while she tapped her keyboard and frowned at her computer screen. After a while, she swiveled the screen around. "Here's the painting you were interested in. The one we just sold."

I leaned closer to study the image of "Mountain High." It was an impressionistic study in lavenders and greens. Snow-capped mountain peaks formed a backdrop, a single house stood in the middle ground, and a field of green filled the foreground. Brushstrokes shaped the leaves in the field like little spears. I recognized that multi-leaf pattern. They were marijuana plants.

And there was more that I recognized. The house stood on stilts against a mountainside. An upper deck and soaring windows were shaped like a boat's prow. I'd seen that house before, on a picnic for some of the university faculty. Jackson James had hosted. Felix's painting showed Jackson's mountain home, I was certain. And Jackson's house came with a marijuana field.

Mountain High.

Six

AFTER LUNCH, I race-walked the few blocks from the karate studio to the address on the *Creations by Erica* label. Might as well grab the extra conditioning while I could.

Through the narrow side yard between houses, I kept glimpsing activity in the alley behind these houses: flashing lights, cops in blue uniforms, and lots of vans. Something was going on, and I didn't think there'd been another fire. Maybe a bear had found a trashcan.

A few minutes later, I found the address of Erica's place. It was another bungalow, like the karate studio, a la turn of the previous century. Except here, the footprint of formal flowerbeds curved graciously around the property. Thistle weeds spiked through overgrown bushes that must've once been flowers. I took several deep breaths and stretched my calf muscles, rocking against the porch steps before continuing on up to the front door. A sign covered the door buzzer, *shhh, baby sleeping*, so I rapped lightly on the screen.

The floor vibrated with scurrying footsteps, and a woman opened a thick wooden door behind the screen. I stiffened with surprise, recognizing her as the same baby-stroller-pushing neighbor who'd yelled at Alice about hash oil the night before.

She'd popped me in the nose. Hers was unbruised and curved like a hawk's beak. Her eyes widened when she recognized me, too. She started to push the door closed, but I was faster.

"You're Erica of *Creations by Erica*?" I said all in one breath, before she could close the door in my face.

She hesitated, and then nodded. "Did you cause the accident in the alley, too?"

"No." I suppressed the urge to laugh at her unreasonable attitude. "Has there been an accident?" So that's what was going on.

"I don't know anything about it. What do you want? Do you have an appointment?" She kept her door open only an inch.

I shook my head. "I've been trying to reach you. The phone must not be working."

"Sometimes I unplug it when the baby's sleeping."

"Could I talk to you? I won't keep you long."

She glanced at her watch and then at my bruised nose. "Then you're not here about your face? What happened last night wasn't my fault, you know."

I nodded. "I know. Are you feeling better today?" Actually, I didn't know. But I didn't want to antagonize her any further. That meant gaining her trust before mentioning Alice by name.

She sniffed. "It was such a shock. That's all. I wouldn't be surprised if that woman started that fire herself to collect the insurance money."

"*Really?*" Here it came. What I'd feared someone would suspect of Alice. But my friend was the world's kindest, gentlest soul. I had to bite my tongue.

Erica went on. "She's not who you think she is. She tried to put me out of business."

A-ha. That could explain why Erica had been so angry at the fire. "I'm here on her behalf," I said. "Do you have a few minutes?"

Erica hesitated and glanced over her shoulder at the dark interior of a shadowy hallway that I couldn't see behind her. "The baby's asleep right now. I don't want to wake her, because with little Charlie in Kiddie Kamp, naptime is my only time to get anything done around here. I'm laying out a new design for a quilt."

"Can we talk inside while you do that?"

It wasn't likely that anyone passing by on the street would be interested in our conversation. Passersby would more likely be curious about the accident in the alley. Or the burned remains of Alice's craft shoppe—oops, I meant *gallery*—which had been splashed across the front page of the newspaper.

Erica shrugged, apparently deciding I was harmless. After all, she'd already gotten my nose. "I guess so." She pushed the screened door open and stood aside for me to enter.

She latched the screen closed behind me but left the wooden front door standing open. I followed her across the entry hall into the dining room, stepping around some sort of baby-mobile and a line-up of toy cars.

"Watch your step," she said, heading straight to the table where swatches of fabric and cut out patterns of animal shapes covered the surface. "I told Charlie to pick up his things this morning, but we were running late."

"No problem." Even if she had asked me if I wanted anything to drink, I didn't. Now that I'd gained entrance, I got straight to the point. "Has Alice Albright contacted you recently?"

"Why on earth would she?"

"She left behind your contact information, and um..." I thought fast. I didn't want to fuel this woman's anger towards Alice. Alice had enough trouble, being interrogated by the police. "I haven't seen her in a while, and I'd like to know that everything's all right. After last night. You know."

"Don't worry about her. She can take care of herself. She's probably on the run. It's about time she got her just desserts."

Whoa. I took a step backwards, putting extra distance from this woman's hostility. "Because you think she tried to put you out of business?"

"I don't *think*, lady, I *know*." Picking up her sewing shears, she punctuated her opinion with a wave of her weapon.

I shifted my weight out of relaxed stance to the balls of my feet, so that I could move quickly if it came down to that. Cautiously, I said, "How did that happen?"

Erica snorted. "By stealing my baby quilts and then commissioning someone else to produce more of them at a lower price."

"You displayed your goods at her shoppe...I mean, gallery?"

"I used to, until she stole my husband."

I stumbled, wavering down from the balls of my feet. Were we talking about the same Alice?

In the flash of an instant, I thought I saw pain crease Erica's face. I relaxed my guard just a bit. "Oh no, I'm...sorry about that."

Erica laughed, but it wasn't a happy sound. "Don't be. Not your fault. But that wasn't enough for the bitch."

A chill crept down the back of my neck upon hearing the b-word.

Erica kept steaming. "On top of all that, she started cheating me out of my commission, and so I figured I could just sell my line of baby gear myself and keep all the profits. Not that there's much profit to pocket, but still, every penny helps, know what I mean?" She swept the sewing shears in a circle around her, indicating the threadbare rug and the table and chairs. All of it was second-hand, judging from the chips and scratches in the wood veneer.

"I can't believe Alice would deliberately cheat you."

"Believe it. When I complained, she claimed it was the new girl's fault. Alice was training a new girl to keep her records, and the kid hadn't learned how to keep track of my inventory. Besides that, she was always high on something. Edibles, probably."

One eyebrow shot up, but I shouldn't be surprised. Food snacks laced with marijuana were readily available now. "You're sure about that?"

"Sure I'm sure. They're selling them in the store on the side. Under the counter, so to speak. 'Meditation Mints'. Didn't you know?"

I felt the color drain from my face as I shook my head no. Alice's shoppe did not have a license for that.

"I would deliver my items to the store," Erica said, not giving me a chance to question her credibility, "and then they just disappeared. That stoned-out new girl claimed she never saw them. Never logged them into the system. You ask me, Alice was in on it. She gave the girl so many edibles she didn't know what was going on, and then she sold them and pocketed all the money herself. She probably hired the new girl to be her scapegoat. That is so like Alice, to shift the blame off onto someone else."

That didn't sound like the Alice I knew. I didn't know

anything about Robinette, the "new girl" in training, other than being the college-aged sister of one of my students. But I had never seen her stoned when she dropped off Elliott or picked him up from karate. It was hard to believe that she could be stoned enough to make such serious mistakes about keeping Alice's records. Or that Alice would condone it, let alone provide edibles to an underage employee. Erica was either lying or sadly misinformed. She had to be.

"What did Alice tell you," I asked, "when you pointed this out to her?"

Erica sniffed. "She said she'd pay me whatever I thought she owed me, but she couldn't pay me anything until she got the money."

That sounded more than fair, if it was true. Alice would give Erica the benefit of the doubt, even if Erica had been lying. This angry mother apparently didn't have any qualms about cheating Alice by overstating what she was owed. I hated to make such a rapid judgment, but with the woman's negativity, I thought that was entirely possible. "What do you think Alice meant by that? How was she going to get the money?"

"You figure it out. I'm just saying, that fire was pretty convenient, wasn't it? Maybe the insurance will pay off her debts now."

"Does Alice have other debts, do you think?"

"Besides her inventory? Well, there's always something with a house. And Alice likes to live above her means."

"She inherited the house from Mrs. Harris. It would've been paid off." Although, property tax didn't come cheap.

"But that's just the thing, isn't it? Why would Mrs. Harris leave the house to *her*? And why did the old lady conveniently die all of a sudden, when she'd always been healthy as a horse? I thought it was interesting that *my* ex moved in with Alice less than a week after Mrs. Harris's funeral."

The stolen husband.

"Your ex?" The only person who'd lived in the same house with Alice, as far as I knew, was the artist, and a body bag had been carried out of the house with his name on it.

"He wasn't just my ex," Erica said, "he was my gardener, too. With him gone, this place has gone to seed."

"You don't mean Felix Todd?"

Erica nodded.

I sputtered some more. "You and Felix...?"

Now I understood some of the reason behind Erica's negativity, and why it had caught Alice in its snare.

Erica was jealous of Alice.

She clutched her sewing scissors, pointing them at me, and said, "None of it would've happened if it hadn't been for LePuc's."

My heart skipped a beat. "LePuc's?"

"LePuc's Culinary Arts. It's a cooking school."

I knew what it was. I had just been there, little more than an hour ago. It's where Max and Jackson had taken classes. It was run by Felix's best friend, Dominic. I had an appointment with him in a few hours.

Erica must not have noticed my distress, because she raced on, growing angrier with each word. "That's where they met. But I say 'good riddance'. All of that is past. Now I'm happily married to someone else, the father of my children. Well, the baby, that is. That jerk Felix was far too interested in his art to ever want a family. You ask me, the two of them deserved each other."

"Wait," I said, trying to process her information that wasn't adding up to me. "You're saying Felix met Alice at *LePuc's*?"

"You deaf, or something?"

I sputtered, trying to catch up to these implications. Alice was at LePuc's, too? She never told me that. Nor about her alleged relationship with Felix. Cautiously, I said, "What are you implying?"

"That maybe she had some help putting away Mrs. Harris so she could inherit the house. Things ran smoothly for them until she and her lover boy had a fight. Maybe he was going to turn her in. And so she had to get rid of him."

"Those are pretty serious allegations."

"I know he's dead. The police were here before you. I say, it's just like Felix to die, to get out of paying child support. The courts ruled that he's responsible for Charlie, after all."

The sound of a baby crying made her look up from her cutting. Erica sent me an exasperated glare as if she blamed me for everything, including waking up the baby.

"I'll just let myself out," I said, tiptoeing back to the door, feeling as if I walked on a bed of burning coals.

At least I had confirmation, of sorts. It *was* Felix who'd died in the fire.

Seven

THE AFTERNOON wore on as the fans hummed, working to clear the air from the karate studio. Alice still hadn't come back from her little chat with the police. She must have plenty of things to do. She was a grown woman. She didn't owe me any explanations of her whereabouts. But I had plenty of questions for her. And I couldn't help worrying. A phone call would've been nice.

I knew she had a cell phone. Who didn't these days? But I didn't know the number offhand. I would have to check to see if she was in my contact list. I used my phone as little as possible.

I kept my phone in the mystery bookstore bag upstairs on the coat rack just inside my apartment door, for quick access on my way out.

I headed up there now, scooped up the bag, and carried it to the futon to paw through its contents for my cell phone.

Sammy squeaked at me from her ferret condo.

"Hey, sleepyhead, you want to prowl?" In two steps I was at her condo, unlatching its tiny metal door. She lay in her hammock, eyeballing me as I returned to the futon and resumed my search.

Darn, Alice wasn't in my contact list. I tucked the phone

back into my bag, pulled out the shiny *Creations by Erica* label, and held it up for the ferret to see.

The hammock creaked as Sammy flipped over.

"You want this for your collection of treasures, do you?" I asked.

Sammy slinked out of her condo, crept to my side, stretched up from her haunches, and sniffed at the label between my fingers.

"You wouldn't happen to know anything about this, big girl? You're the one who put it in my bag in the first place, aren't you?"

Sammy reached for it.

"Not so fast." I carried the label to the kitchen corner and tucked it on a shelf inside an upper cabinet, out of Sammy's reach. Through the window, I could see movement next door as investigators continued to sift through the remains of Alice's house. I wondered if they had found the fireproof box of cash Jackson had been looking for. Alice had acted as if she didn't even know about it. How would Jackson have known?

I headed back downstairs to the workout floor. Students would be arriving soon for the first class of the day. I turned off the fan and sniffed the air. It still smelled smoky in here. Not good. I didn't relish the idea of asking my tight-wad boss to send remediators over to clean the studio.

I turned the fan back on and continued across the floor to the office in back and its antique gold telephone.

Poppy, the receptionist my boss shared with several other offices in his building, picked up on the fifth ring. Either she'd been doing her nails again or flirting. I guessed the latter, as I heard a muffled giggle before she launched into her receptionist's greeting.

"Hey, Poppy, it's Nell. Is Mr. Callahan in?"

She squealed and dropped the phone. When she came back on the line she said, "Isn't it terrible, what happened? Only next door to the karate studio, gosh! How's the studio? How are *you*?"

"That's why I'm calling. We're going to need some remediators in here to clean the place to get rid of the smoke smell. May I speak to Mr. Callahan?"

"Well, you could, except he's not here. I've been trying to reach him, too, but you know how he is. Very hard to reach unless he wants to be reached. But don't worry. He'll check in. He always does. Maybe in another day or two."

"If he read the papers this morning, he'll already know about the fire."

"That's just the thing. He wouldn't have. He's away on vacation. He's gone fishing."

"*Fishing?*" Granted, I didn't know my boss well, not after five months of running the studio for him, but I couldn't picture the entrepreneur trading in his tweed sport coat for fishing waders.

"Oh, he's a big fisherman," Poppy said.

"What do you know? Well, darn. I just wanted to get his approval for canceling classes while we bring in the remediators. Inhaling smoke doesn't make for the best environmental conditions for exercising."

"Remember why he hired *you*, Nell. You have to take initiative and do what needs to be done. He doesn't like to be bothered by details."

"Right." I took that as good-enough approval, and we rang off. Although, why Callahan had hired me in the first place, over younger, more athletic martial artists, still remained a mystery.

Not that I was complaining. I'd desperately needed a job when Max walked out on me, draining most of our joint savings account. I hadn't had a lot of options with my half-page, outdated resume.

The smoke in the studio wasn't all that bad, but I'd had to play it up to sound convincing enough to hire remediators. I did not want to scrub the walls and clean the carpet myself.

But it looked like I was going to have to. I couldn't pay for professional cleaners, and I couldn't wait for Callahan and his credit card to return, either. I didn't dare use my plastic, not with my bank balance.

As students started to arrive, class turned into an optional clean-the-studio workout drill. They were happy to oblige. Martial arts kids—the ones who stayed on—were the best, most agreeable, most cooperative kids ever. Adults, too, as they wanted to serve as positive role models. Those who weren't obliging, eventually weeded themselves out. The program was too strenuous for slackers to keep up with it.

Those students who stayed here to help, pulled down the memorabilia and gear from the walls where I had hung stuff to make the little bungalow feel more like a real martial arts studio. There were rainbow colors of belts, framed photographs, certificates, the American and Korean flags, and of course a poster with the black belt creed printed on it. Students had to memorize the creed and follow it as their code of behavior. Their goal was to attain the black belt spirit through honesty and respect. They worked on it, stacking the gear into boxes and carrying them all back to the office. They had to bow onto and off the floor with each trip. After fifty minutes of this activity, we lined up, recited our creed, and bowed out. The next class, waiting in the wings, lined up, bowed in, and took the previous students' places. Some of them started scrubbing the walls, and others carried punching bags outside to air out.

Alice still hadn't showed up by the time Terra returned from her day at band camp. I gave Terra two tasks: 1) Find someone in the neighborhood who might have actually known Mrs. Harris, the elderly lady Alice had served as companion. I wanted to find out the true state of her health, either confirming or rejecting Erica's opinion. And 2) to phone up my students. Terra always excelled at any task dealing with phone work. I hoped that would carry over to the required diplomacy for the Mrs. Harris task.

I gave Terra a list of my students' names and their phone numbers. She started calling them to give them the message that classes would be cancelled the rest of today (unless they wanted to come in and help clean the studio) and all of tomorrow. I hoped that would give me enough time to get the studio back in order. We only had forty-eight students in this *dojo*, total, so Terra should be able to call most of them in a reasonable amount of time. Of course I had to bribe her with a bonus in her allowance.

During one of the breaks between "classes," when my student crew shifted, Terra caught me by the sleeve of my T-shirt and asked if I'd seen Kitti Kandi. Frankly, I hadn't given much thought to the cat, since my mind was filled with other matters, including Alice's whereabouts.

No, I didn't know where either of them was. As I returned to the workout floor, I heard an exchange of voices, and they lifted a little too vehemently. Elliott, my squeaky-wheel twelve-year-old orange belt whose sister had alerted us about the fire, lifted a sponge in one hand as if it were a weapon.

"Does not!" he shouted, or maybe cried.

The scrawny, tall green belt next to him, a kid named Blake, sidestepped the sponge and chuckled.

Chanel, the diligent organizer, grabbed Elliott's arm. "Don't listen to him."

I tagged all three of them and said, "Follow me." I led them along the edge of the workout floor, down the curving hall to my office and nodded at the conference table. "Have a seat, you three."

The green belt lifted his eyebrows. "Uh-oh."

Terra looked up from her position by the phone. "I think I'll take a break." She headed out the back door, leaving me alone with my three students.

"It wasn't me, Ms. Letterly," Chanel said, tripping over her tongue. "It was him!" She stabbed one finger at Blake. "And I told him he'd get us in trouble."

I sent them a warning look. "Who wants to tell me what's going on?"

"Nothing's going on," Elliott said, folding his arms against his chest. His lower lip stuck out and quivered.

Blake grinned. "That's what you think."

"Elliott's right," Chanel said. "Because you're just making it up."

"You punks don't pay attention," Blake said with a laugh.

"Hold on," I said. "Black belts treat everyone with respect. Our studio is a no-name-calling zone."

"Whatever." Blake slouched in his chair and twisted away from us.

I bit my tongue and squeezed the chrome edge of the table to keep from smacking the kid. "Remember our creed and our goals to black belt: through honesty and respect."

Elliott flounced on his seat, squeaking its vinyl cushion. "I do too know! And you're wrong about Robinette." He turned to me. "Ms. Letterly, Blake thinks my sister is some sort of drug dealer."

Blake snorted. "Not dealer, you goof. Marijuana courier. That means she delivers the stuff. Money, too."

Elliott ignored him and kept talking at me. I heard the wheedling earnestness in his voice, trying to persuade me to his way of thinking. "He thinks one of her deals went wrong, and they're going to blame her for the fire next door, but he's wrong."

I studied the green belt in question and the smudges of dirt along the hem of his white karate pants. I waited for him to speak, but he shook his head and stared at his bare toes tapping a pattern against the black-and-white checkered floor.

Finally I said, "Blake? Did she tell you she's a courier?" He shook his head, and I went on. "Then, why do you think that?"

"'Cause it's true."

"No way!" Chanel said with a yelp.

"Do you have any evidence?" I said.

"I don't have to. Everyone knows that. Besides, I've seen her out in the alley with that guy in the hat."

"The guy in the hat?" I frowned and remembered Jackson's Panama hat. Jackson was a guy in a hat.

Or maybe he meant the guy in the fedora, that guy whom Gillian swore was spying on us while we ate lunch on the mall. He was up to no good.

"Sure," Blake said. "Some older guy. He made her his contact. She's delivering weed for him, and they make the deals right next door."

"But why would they do that," I asked, "when there are lots of places to buy the stuff legally?" I did not want to be having this conversation with my students, but I had to get to the bottom of this matter if I was going to provide a safe environment for them.

"Because."

I didn't think Blake was going to go on, not the way his foot tapping progressed. Now his entire leg bounced up and down.

"Because why?"

"I dunno, not personally, y'know? But I think some people want something a little different. A little weird. For a different kind of high."

"You're wrong," Chanel said. "She wouldn't do that. She can't. She's not old enough."

"And besides," Elliott said, "they wouldn't try to burn the house down for that."

"Maybe someone would to put her out of business," Blake said. "Haven't any of you noticed what's been going on right next door to the karate studio?"

This last question seemed especially aimed at me. If Blake was right, then I wondered if I was completely blind.

"Mr. Valencia knew all about it," Blake said for a final jab.

I had no doubt. I could easily believe that my ill-fated predecessor had attempted to ruin the studio by being involved in something underhanded. But Alice? What role did Alice play in all this? Before I could respond, Elliott nearly rocketed out of his chair.

"You think you know everything, but you don't!" he said. "Robinette first started going over there because that artist was giving her paint lessons. It wasn't for the weed! She knew I always wanted to take karate, and when she saw this place next door to where she painted, she told me about it, and so I enrolled here. But she stopped taking classes from him after he made her cry, and Alice gave her a job, instead."

"Wait," I said. "Felix Todd? The *artist*? He made your sister cry?" I wondered what it would take to make her cry. The night of the fire she'd done a lot of crying.

"Right. I guess he made fun of what she painted. He wasn't very nice. That's what Robi said."

"Lucky thing that Alice was nice to her," Chanel said.

Lucky, indeed. But where was Alice now? And how much else was she keeping from me?

Eight

I SHOOED THE REST of my students out of the karate studio, left Terra in charge, and headed over to LePuc's for my appointment with Max's chef. Dominic. It beat me as to why—maybe because my intuition, aka suspicion, had scored—but I was shaking like a nervous schoolgirl on her first prom date.

This time the door was unlocked. It gave a fraction of a slit as I leaned against it. I leaned harder and called through the gap in the open door. "Hello?"

Ms. Sunshine did not sing out to me in response. I stepped across the reception area to her chest-high counter, but no one sat hidden behind the half-wall that protected her desk. Beyond her desk was the classroom, also empty. Barstools for student stations lined an L-shaped countertop facing a demo area with cooktop and sink. A sliver of daylight streamed from a back room, an office of some sort, into this windowless meeting space. A shadow moved back there, and someone's heels clicked and squeaked across a hard, tile surface. The sounds echoed against the rafters of the empty meeting space.

"Hello?" I called louder, pushing my way forward to one of the barstools.

The outline of a darkened figure paused in the lit doorway. "Sorry, but class doesn't start for another hour," said a man's voice, oddly lilting for his hefty size.

"I have an appointment with one of the chefs."

"You will have to do better than that. We have several chefs here."

"Dominic LePuc. Can you tell me where I might find him?"

"*C'est moi*," he said, stepping closer in his squeaky patent leather shoes. His accent sounded fake French to me. "But I do not recall granting an appointment with anyone for this hour."

I circled around to where the light filtering in from his back office hit his pudgy cheeks, his beady eyes, and his receding hairline. What was left of his coarse and wavy black hair shone, as if pampered with mousse. I'd seen him before. I was sure. Had it been with Max? I searched my memory of those days but came up empty. "I stopped in earlier today, and the receptionist said I should come back now."

He sighed, a long and drawn out sound of exasperation. His hands, wrapped in surgical gloves, flung upwards, as if invoking the gods of the rafters. "She has no right to schedule appointments for me, and she always forgets to lock the door. But you are here now. What can I do for you? It will have to be quick. My class arrives in less than an hour, yes?"

Quick, I could not do. It was complicated. Where to start? As usual, I jumped in, without thinking properly about the consequences. "My, uh, husband and his friend took a class here called 'making the impossible soufflé possible'."

"I remember it well. A complete disaster. We will not be offering it again, I am afraid, not unless there is demand for it in another year or so. I am doing flambéing in the next session, one of our more popular classes, and rightly so. So if you like crème brulee, then you must sign up online. I believe there is still room."

"It's not for me."

"I see. For your husband, then?"

"Not exactly. Do you remember him? His name is Max Gannon."

"Ah. I see. Now I remember. He is that chap who disappeared a while ago, is he not? A professor, or something? And you are the wife?" He narrowed his eyes to ferret-sized nuggets and looked me up and down.

"Technically. But not for much longer. I heard that he might be coming back to town, and I thought if that's true, he might contact you." Not in so many words, but it was sort of true.

"My dear lady, what gives you such an idea? I hardly know him. Why should he contact me? What exactly are you insinuating? Surely he has much closer associates who might give him assistance, if that is what he seeks."

Like Jackson.

"If you see him, tell him my lawyer's looking for him."

He spread flour on his chin as he thought some more. "Now that you mention it, that would explain things, would it not? I never took him for a thief, but a thief he must be. I recall that he always admired my favorite chef's knife, and now it has gone missing."

Many things Max was, but aside from helping himself to my share of our joint savings account, he was not a common thief. This was the father of my child, regardless of his errant ways. I pressed on. "I understand you knew Felix Todd."

He frowned and rubbed his temple, thinking, as he smudged flour across his brow. "The name is familiar. Sorry. I cannot remember all of my students. They come and go."

"He's not a friend of yours?"

He clucked his tongue and shook his head. "A friend? No. A student, perhaps."

"How about Jackson James? Do you remember him?"

"Another student? Perhaps." He harrumphed. "Talk to one of them, if you wish my references."

"What about Alice Albright?"

I swear I caught a flicker of recognition, or surprise, in the twitching scowls that creased his face. Apparently, the angry Erica had been right about Alice meeting Felix here.

I pressed on. "I understand that you were the only one that Felix Todd allowed into his inner sanctum of his artist's garret."

The thick black line of his eyebrows rose like a lid from an exploding pot. "Certainly not. Where do you understand a thing like that?" One hand spiraled upwards and the other hand knuckled ominously against his hip.

Okay, my conclusion had made a leap. Maybe there *was* another Dominic in town. But judging from his overreaction—alarm?—I thought not. Shifting my weight to the balls of my feet and keeping his fists in sight, I said cautiously, "You deny knowing Felix as a friend?"

"Why do you come in here asking such outrageous questions?"

"Alice Albright lost her house last night to a fire where Felix rented his studio and—" I bit my tongue before adding "died." The press would inform Dominic soon enough about Felix's death.

"And you think that fire was more than just an unfortunate accident?"

"I think my friend Alice needs my help."

"And that gives you the right to barge in here and fling

102

accusations right and left?"

Color flushed my cheeks. Had I been too hasty? I couldn't remember making any accusations, but maybe that's how my questions had sounded. I was verging into whine territory. I knew what Alice had told me. This man was lying. Perhaps, for the sake of his cooking school, it was important to him to distance himself from any potential scandal.

"Sorry," I said. "I only wanted to help my friend, and your place, this cooking school, keeps coming up in the conversation. There's a girl, you see, who works for Alice and also works here, a young lady going to college. I am told that she has I don't know how many part-time jobs—"

"You're speaking of Robinette. She's my daughter."

My mind reeled. Robinette was my student Elliott's sister, but I did not remember seeing Dominic LePuc's name on any of Elliott's registration forms as his father. Elliott's last name was different. They must be half-siblings.

I sank down from the balls of my feet and tried to make sense of this new piece of information. Then I remembered where I'd seen Dominic before. He'd been helping at the scene of the fire as the self-appointed cop before the real cops arrived. He'd been helping his *daughter*.

Nine

I HADN'T SEEN IT coming. All the way across town, back to the karate studio, I pondered Robinette's work ethic. Everywhere I turned, her name kept popping up. Then again, Boulder felt smaller and smaller, despite the intentions of relentless developers like Jimmie Condo. We were no longer an overgrown waystation to the mountains, a blossoming supply town to the gold mines. We were swiftly being Californicated.

And speaking of California exiles, where was Alice?

By the time I returned to the karate studio, she still hadn't. Time to find out about her day with my cop pals.

Before I could reach the phone, Terra intercepted me.

"Gramps is mad," she said. "He's been calling here all night. Wants you to call him back."

"Did he say what it's about?"

"He said you'd know. So give, Mom. What's up?"

"Honey, I wish I knew. I've got to make another call first. And then we have to get you to Aunt Jill's. Gramps will have to wait."

My dad did not wait well, but I was convinced he'd understand, once I had a chance to explain everything.

I was in luck. Hennesey answered the phone himself, rather than going to his voicemail. This cop didn't seem to ever go off-duty.

105

Of course not. He hadn't finished interviewing Alice yet.

"Good evening, Ms. Letterly," he said. He was such a nice, cooperative cop, unlike his partner. "What can I do for you?"

Keep keeping your partner away from me, I thought. Instead I said, "I am wondering when my neighbor, Alice Albright can come home."

Silence.

"Hello? Detective? Are you still there?"

"Um, yes. Ms. Albright left here several hours ago. I'm just finishing up my reports now."

"But she hasn't returned home yet. Do you know where she went?"

"I'm sorry, but no. I don't know."

I felt my heart clench, the same way it did when Terra stayed out late with friends. "Was she okay when she left there?" I hoped she wasn't so upset that she would've done something foolish, something that would've gotten her into trouble, something like...

I had no idea what she might do. I didn't really know her. I *thought* I knew her, but maybe I was wrong. I didn't know what to think. Maybe I hadn't known her at all.

"Understandably," Hennesey said, "she was upset about the victim's identity."

"It was Felix Todd, right?"

More silence. Finally, he said, "The DNA report isn't back yet."

"Meaning, I'm not supposed to know. It's okay, you don't have to tell me. I can guess."

It couldn't have been anyone else. I remembered what Jackson had told me, about the way he admired Felix Todd the artist. But it must've gone farther than mere admiration, since Jackson knew that Felix kept money in a fireproof box. And now Jackson thought someone was after him for that. Jackson and Felix must've been partners in something, I concluded. Maybe it was something to do with marijuana, as my student Blake had suggested.

"Do you know yet how the fire started?" I asked.

"It seems to have been an accident."

"Because of Felix's negligence? So, he started it himself? Accidentally? He was probably using flammable stuff with his paints, right?"

"Ms. Letterly, you have been helpful in the past, but I suggest you let the authorities handle the investigation. And in the meanwhile, please don't talk to any journalists. The press has been nosing around. We don't have a statement ready for them yet, and we don't want false information to spread."

"Sure, no sweat." Ever since Max's disappearance, some reporters thought we had a chummy relationship. We didn't. I hadn't exactly been on friendly terms with the press.

"And another thing," Hennesey said. "Make certain you keep your doors and windows locked."

"I always do." Hennesey's scolding didn't have the same sting that his partner's had had, and I was grateful for that. But still, it troubled me that there was apparently something he wasn't telling me.

* * * * *

I scribbled a note saying I'd be back in ten minutes, in case Alice returned while Terra and I were out, and taped it to the door. In truth, it'd be closer to half an hour, but I didn't want to give any would-be burglars an invitation for a leisurely break-in. Terra shoved Sammy into her backpack, already packed with jammies and toothbrush, and we headed out into the alley toward the Ghia.

A late summer night was falling, throwing shadows everywhere, shadows made thicker by the nearness of the mountains. In this mix of residential and commercial, someone's sprinkler went thwik-tchik-thwik in the petunia-scented air of a backyard garden. And there was another sound. Leaves swished from the depths of darkening shadows. But the air was still. No breeze had rattled any leaves. I grabbed Terra by the elbow, and we jerked to a stop at the graveled edge of our parking space.

"Kitti Kandi?" I said hopefully. "Is that you?" But the cat didn't show her face any more than Alice had. I paused for a heartbeat and then lunged for the car. "Get in the car," I told Terra, stabbing my key into the antique slot. Dang, I wished I had a newer car, nothing fancy, just something with a remote clicker to unlock it. I cursed Max under my breath once again, this time for his love of antique cars. He'd found this one for me years ago, but its sportiness had faded long past its prime.

Terra and I both dove into the bucket seats, slammed and locked the doors, and stared at the mass of dark shrubbery sprawling between the perimeter of the alley and the shed. Behind the shed, Alice's burned shell of a house rose like smudged fingers against the twilight sky.

Terra turned to me. "Do you think that's the bear? My friend Jason says there was a bear only a block away from us last week. What if it's come *here*?"

I turned the ignition and flipped on the headlights. True,

we had a history of bears in town, especially in garbage-can-infested alleys, in spite of our new supposedly bear-proof trashcans, but I didn't want to feed Terra's alarm. "Probably it was just a raccoon."

"Or a mountain lion," Terra said in a slightly higher register.

Bushes stood motionless beside the shed. If the rustling movement was from wildlife, then whatever it was would lope out of the bushes, frightened by our lights. It would, wouldn't it?

Nothing came out of the bushes.

So I guessed it wasn't a bear. Whatever it was, it wasn't frightened of us. Or else it was deliberately hiding from us. Either way, that made the swishing sounds all the more ominous.

"We can't leave Kandi outside overnight," Terra said. "Maybe we should wait some more for Alice to get back. We can go to Aunt Jill's later, can't we? What's the rush?"

"You need to get to bed, young lady."

She flounced in her seat. "A little more time won't hurt. It's not like band camp is school, or anything. Bri gets to stay up past eleven. And Kelsey —"

I crunched the gears and backed out of the parking space, then crunched some more. We spewed gravel, lurching into the alley. Terra fell silent.

What a nuisance! I was going to have to come back here, after dropping Terra at Gillian's, and wait for Alice. If she ever showed up—no, make that *when* she finally showed—I'd give her a piece of my mind. Of course I'd never really do that, but how rude of her. I almost regretted having offered her my couch. But since I had offered it, I couldn't back out now, much as I wished I could. I had to keep my end of the deal.

But I'd already spent most of the day waiting for her, so if she returned while I was out, then she could just wait for me, for a change. Egged on by my snarky mood, I bounced the car over the potholes, and we puttered out onto the pavement of the street. There were almost as many potholes out here on these side streets as in the alleys. Road crews were running out of summer to fill them.

Max's half-sister Gillian Gannon lived in an upscale townhouse on a quiet residential street with more clout and fewer potholes. A five-minute drive away from us, her house was just a few blocks west of the downtown pedestrian mall (for easy access to clubbing) and just a few blocks east of the mountains that backdropped Boulder. Gillian once confessed that living so close to the mountains made her feel like a western cowgirl. She wasn't. She'd come out here from a very proper east-coast upbringing, financed by old-style family wealth.

Gillian greeted us at her door with a green masque drying on her face. The green matched the color of her eyes, and it also matched the headband holding back her blonde hair. "*Here* you are, *fiii*-nally," she said with a harrumph. "I was about to give up on you."

Her jade gaze fluttered down to her toes, where bits of foam wedged between them. Three toenails displayed plum pink paint, matching her terrycloth robe. Gillian was all about matching. She hobbled on her heels, leading us down the hall to the family room at the back of the townhouse, where a heavy smell of cosmetics hung in the air. She swooped down onto a footstool and delicately retrieved a bottle of nail polish from the gleaming wood surface of her Queen Anne side table. Terra followed along like a pet lamb. You could almost hear her mental typewriter clacking away as she keenly observed and took note of every movement made by her beloved Aunt Jill.

"Have you managed to track down a painting yet, for the family?" Gillian said, dabbing more pink onto her toes.

"What painting?" Terra's eyes grew wider as she glanced between Gillian and me.

I figured it was time she knew about our mystery, so I updated them both, giving them the PG version of angry Erica's tale.

It only took about ninety seconds for us to reach our conclusions: 1) Terra said that obviously (with an eye roll) the boyfriend from California had set the fire as a sort of revenge against Alice. Terra offered to go online and find out what she could about him. 2) Gillian, who was overdue for a new romance in her life, volunteered to pursue Jimmie Condo and find out more about his offer to buy out Alice for a development. 3) I said that Robinette knew more than what she let on. My challenge would be to catch up to her busy schedule.

With our tasks decided upon, I returned home to the karate studio. No one waited for me on either the front or back porch. So. Alice was still gone. I searched inside the karate studio, and I even climbed the stairs and unlocked my apartment, just in case Alice had somehow managed to find her way in. She was not there.

I ran back downstairs and stepped out onto the front porch. "Here, kitty, kitty, kitty."

Kandi did not step out of the dark. I closed, locked, and bolted the front door, and then sped through the studio to the back porch. "Here, kitty, kitty, kitty."

No meow responded. Not even the bushes rustled in

response, as they had done before.

I sighed, thinking this was bad news for Kandi. I locked up the back, too, but I could neither go to bed nor head back to Gillian's place. Alice would return at any moment. Maybe Kandi was hiding in a bush, waiting for her. I sat down at my desk, flicked on the reading light, and picked up the latest mystery novel I'd found in the library. Brain candy for the mind.

A chapter and a half in, a dog started barking from the student apartments across the alley from the karate studio. It wouldn't shut up. Being the official caretaker here—it was in my contract, and that's why Callahan had offered me the apartment upstairs free of rent—I had to check it out and see if everything was all right.

It wasn't.

When I flipped on the outdoor lights, I saw the shadow of a figure moving along the alley. The slinking way he moved, with the outline of a hat pulled down low over his head made him (or her?) appear that this was not just an innocent, nighttime stroll. Maybe he was Robinette's contact that Blake had told us about. Or the "suspicious-looking character" Jackson had been worried about, someone looking for his money in the fireproof box.

At least the shadow was moving away from me. I closed the door and locked it shut, then camped out in the kitchen office with my book until daybreak.

Ten

THE BEEP OF AN incoming text message startled me awake. I had dozed off in my chair, with my book fanned out on the floor, my page lost.

Gillian: *See pg B1*

I'd deliberately left my phone turned on, since Terra was away at Gillian's.

I hauled myself out of my chair, staggered down the hall and through the studio to the front door, and peered out the side window before unbolting it. Nothing. No one. I crept out to fetch the morning paper, which the paper carrier had tossed into the two-foot space between the public sidewalk and my porch steps.

Back inside, I ripped open the bagged roll of newspaper and found page B1. "Man Found Dead on Hill." It was a brief article in a side column, no more than a paragraph, describing a car accident in an alley on the Hill, leaving one man dead. No identification given. No determination yet if drugs or alcohol had played a part.

A-ha. That had to be the story that had set Gillian off. Another death in *That Place*. It didn't matter that it was an accident. It was another reason why Terra and I shouldn't be here. On the Hill.

I wondered if this was also the story behind the flashing lights of the patrol cars yesterday in the alley behind Erica's house, just up the street from here. I brewed some coffee and carried my mug outside to the picnic table to ponder the meaning of another day. The crystal clear air tasted fresh this morning, with only a slight hint of ash.

I had learned that I could always find "meaning" somewhere in the philosophy of martial arts. Winning in the martial arts is all about attitude. The competitor with the fiercest attitude always gets the judges' attention, often times at the cost of overlooking skill.

It's the same with squeaky wheels. I had a handful of them as students—three or four (or five, if you count the one who is no longer a student at my *dojo*, but that's another story) out of fifty students (forty-eight, to be exact, but I expected a pair of siblings to sign up in the next week or two—their complimentary lessons had gone well). In other words, about ten percent of my students took up about ninety percent of my time instructing on account of their squeakiness.

Parents were another matter.

Attitude—or a lack thereof—was the reason Hennesey and I got along so well. He wasn't like his absent partner, Rosenquist, my cop-nemesis with an attitude so fierce it scared the socks off me. So when Hennesey told me not to do something, like "don't investigate the fire next door that killed Felix," I thanked him for his advice and went about my business as if he hadn't spoken. I wasn't going to let Hennesey intimidate me.

My students were *my* business. Not Hennesey's. And that included my students' families. One certain sister came to mind, along with three puzzle pieces that Elliott's squeakiness made me determined to fit together.

1. Robinette had seemed more than just distressed when fire broke out next door. She'd almost seemed panic-stricken. I couldn't help but wonder why.

2. And then there was Robinette's alleged use of marijuana, both as a pothead (as accused by Erica) and her work as a marijuana courier (as accused by Blake). Apparently, I was the only one left in the world who did not know any of this.

3. On top of all that, Elliott said that Felix the artist had made his sister cry when he humiliated her.

And speaking of Elliott brought to mind a fourth puzzle piece: Robinette's parentage. Dominic might be Robinette's father, but he was not Elliott's, according to my student's enrollment papers. I'd verified that.

The sum of the parts came out to a total that made me squirm and fidget with crawlie sensations under my T-shirt and shorts. I desperately needed to talk to Robinette, despite Hennesey's pansy attempt of a scolding, and find out for myself what the heck was going on. I couldn't allow one sibling's troubles to worry the rest of my students.

I phoned Elliott's house (was this Dominic's house, too?) and asked to speak to Robinette.

She wasn't there. In fact, she didn't even live with the family anymore, not now that she was a university student. Part-time, but still. If I hurried, Elliott told me over the phone, I could probably catch her at her current housesitting job.

As it turned out, the address of that job placed her in my old neighborhood. Robinette was sitting for someone only a couple blocks away from the suburban house I'd shared with Max.

If I hurried... But the studio still had to air out, and I still had to clean the carpet. Fun. Classes were scheduled to resume tomorrow. There was no rush.

I showered and dressed.

On my way out, a pitiful meow floated down from the treetops and stopped me in my tracks. I looked up. The cottonwood leaning close to the upper floor of Alice's house had lost a lot of leaves in the fire. The few that still clung to the tree had curled up and were singed around the edges. One of the branches drooped toward a small triangular rooftop jutting out from Alice's second floor and covering a porch below. Sitting atop the roof was the missing cat, looking quite chagrined. Kandi must've climbed the tree, escaping whatever had startled her below—possibly bear-shaped—and then gotten stuck.

"Kandi? Come on down. You got yourself up there, for goodness sake."

Mew! Me-ewww! The cat was no kitten, but she made kittenish cries of desperation.

Okay. I was a sucker, but I wasn't going to climb that poor, listing tree. I glanced around but saw no fire investigators to help.

Kandi crouched, peering over the edge of the rooftop with wide, Siamese-blue eyes. She pawed the air, where the branch didn't quite touch the roof. Behind the cat was a tiny window over the porch rooftop. It looked as if the window must be positioned on the landing of the stairs inside.

No one was around. I guessed it wouldn't hurt if I just took a quick look inside. I wouldn't actually go *in*. I would just assess the situation, that's all. But maybe—who knew?—just maybe I could find a safe way up to that window to rescue the cat. I was smart enough not to proceed if it looked too dangerous. I couldn't leave the poor, helpless cat stuck.

I ducked under the yellow tape. Blackened bits of unrecognizable debris scattered along the sidewalk and pooled around the brick perimeter of the house. I crunched up onto the concrete porch and spied a large crack between the boards that covered the gaping hole where a door had been. I peeked through, and one board came loose in my hands. I poked my head inside. Black rubble darkened the dim interior. I hadn't expected to see the stairs still standing, but there they were.

Nell, Nell, Master Hwang's voice chided me in my head. *No be stupid.*

I wasn't going to do anything stupid. Really.

The cat meowed again. I pried loose another board and climbed inside. It was hard to breathe in here, as if the residue of the fire had sucked out all the oxygen. I shifted my weight over the balls of my feet and ninja-crept further inside, ready to spring at a moment's notice if anything caved in from above. I focused my gaze straight ahead but looked through my peripheral vision for a 180-degree view.

Wow.

Alice's business, her whole life, had been reduced to charred rubble and ashes. I'd known that intellectually, but seeing it with my own eyes...the debris left behind in the wake of disaster... It touched my core deep inside. The whimsy of natural forces could take away a life's work in the relative blink of an eye. And yet, we struggled on, rebuilding our lives, strengthening ourselves from the inside out.

But Alice had gone through this once before. I couldn't imagine how it would affect her, losing her life's work a second time.

I tested the steps one at a time. They creaked, and with each creak I paused, gradually testing them with more of my weight. They held, and finally I reached the landing.

But the window wouldn't open. I told myself it would be all right to break the glass. Alice would forgive me, in exchange for the cat. And anyway, the entire house would have to be gutted and rebuilt. One more broken pane of glass wouldn't matter. I looked around for some hard piece of debris to break it with and spied a rectangular tin can, the size of Master Hwang's fist and lidded shut. It tucked into one dark corner under the windowsill and rattled when I picked it up. I pried off the lid to reveal bits of colored, broken glass inside. Hmmm. I replaced the lid and let the can rattle as I banged it against the windowpane. It took several bangs and a driving front punch to finally break, tinkling its glass across the landing.

I pocketed the can in my running shorts, so that I could return it later to Alice, and coaxed the cat through the broken window. Clutching her in my arms, I crept cautiously back down the stairs and out the hole in the front door. Kandi immediately jumped from my arms and darted toward the alley, dodging a man in tan slacks who stood on the porch.

"Ms. Letterly," said Detective Hennesey. "What were you doing in there?"

"Obviously, rescuing the cat, Detective. What brings *you* here?"

He ignored my question and deepened his frown. "You knew this site is off limits, and yet you persisted."

He sounded as if he'd been taking lessons from his curmudgeon of a partner.

"True, but I had a good reason." I watched the cat slink

along the alley toward the karate studio. "You should be out looking for Alice, since she still hasn't come back. What did you say to her, for goodness' sake?"

He ignored that, too, as if Alice's absence didn't worry him in the least. "Have any reporters been around yet?"

I shook my head. "Not unless…" Maybe it had been a reporter in the bushes last night. I told Hennesey about the noises I'd heard and about the shadowy person I'd seen strolling down the alley, setting off the neighbor's dog.

He didn't seem concerned, at least not outwardly, much to my exasperation. No wonder I had to solve his case for him. Time was wasting. I excused myself and headed out back to my car. I needed to find Robinette, and I hoped the cat detour hadn't consumed too much time.

In the light of day, scratch marks jumped out of the Ghia's yellow paint job. They hadn't been there last night, coming home from Gillian's. Was this a gift from the shadowy alley visitor? The marks spelled out a single word: *Bitch*.

Me?

I glanced over my shoulder, but no one stood behind me, not even Hennesey, whom I'd left behind at the fire scene. A hair tickled the back of my neck.

Who else was the message intended for but me? It wasn't the first time I'd received such a message.

And yes, if truth be told, I guess I was.

Clearly, I'd made someone nervous.

I suppressed a grin and climbed inside the car.

Maybe, I thought, pulling out of the alley, I'd made someone angry. Someone who was already angry to start with. Someone who'd unintentionally punched me in the nose. Maybe that flailing fist hadn't been an accident. After all, the angry neighbor woman was filled with mega doses of negative energy.

I held my chin up high, the b-lady, and steered out into the traffic of Broadway, the main north-south artery of town. So far, it remained untouched by the driving obstacles that city council's minions constructed, like circles or speed humps or bike lanes. The pocketed can of broken glass pinched my thigh, reminding me that I still had it. Oh darn. Hennesey was going to be really mad at me, but Alice's stranded cat and the b-job on my car had distracted me.

Fifteen minutes later, I pulled up in front of the house where Robinette was house-sitting, slid the can out of my pocket, and tucked it into the glove compartment. I was too late. The house looked all locked up and empty. I rang the bell twice, stirring a dog to bark, but no answer. Dominic's daughter was already gone.

I swiped my hair in frustration. I'd struck out finding Robinette. How was I ever going to catch up to her if she changed jobs faster than most people changed socks?

But now that I'd driven to the north side of town... Maybe I could make my trip across town useful.

As long as I was here in the suburbs, I decided to swing by my old place, the "country estate," some of my karate buddies had teased. It wasn't far from here. As the homeowner, I should periodically make sure the house still stood. I would've heard from the renters if there'd been a problem. Okay, I confessed. I couldn't quite get the old house out of my blood.

It wasn't old, actually, but quite contemporary.

A few minutes later, I pulled into the cul-de-sac and stopped a couple houses away to catch my breath as the ghosts of my past flitted across the lawn. That life had gone away. The person I had been was gone, too.

My house stood silent behind a screen of aspens. With Max's reluctant help, I'd planted a few of them that first summer after we'd bought the house, and now they'd spread into a grove.

A stream of memories played across the grounds of that house like a movie. I saw Ruth, my best friend, hanging a housewarming wreath on the front door, Max and myself sipping cocktails on the verandah back when we used to do that sort of thing. I saw baby Terra in her playpen throwing toys at me as I pulled weeds. Toddlers scattered through aspen saplings on an Easter Egg hunt. Dad was there, too, as an obstinate patient recovering from his heart attack in the lounger. And I saw Terra and me, painting the house ourselves in order to save some money for extra things, like baseball tickets. I bowed my head and blinked back the memories.

I had to move forward with my life, but darn it, I wanted my mother.

You go nowhere when you feel sorry for self, Master Hwang told my subconscious. I was the strongest person available to me.

Okay. I found a tissue and blew my nose.

"Yoo-hoo! Is that really you, Nell?"

Oh heck. Turning, I saw one of my former neighbors running toward me. Celeste. Her hair flapped like a black mat behind her, and her body parts jiggled as she ran across the cul-de-sac. Behind her, the hood of her BMW was propped open. She was dressed in jeans that were fashionably tight on her lithe body and a T-shirt that spelled out the name of the shop from which it had come. An interesting outfit, I thought, for checking your oil.

"You're just the person I needed to see," Celeste said, breathless, when she reached the side of my car.

She was a study in Snow White contrast with ice blue eyes and artificially-heightened black hair. Her skin was a pale shade of iron deficiency. Only, she looked a lot less innocent than the fairy tale princess.

I was about to tell her that I was only passing through and had no time to stop for a chat—I had to get back to work, after all, cleaning the studio—when red splotches broke out on her white face and her eyebrows contorted. "Oh, Nell! I may have to move, too, just the way you did. Ralph's left me."

"Oh no, Celeste. I'm so sorry."

"Sorry? No, I'm the one who's sorry. What am I going to do now? It's all my fault. I don't want a divorce. I love him! I truly do! But no one believes me. Do you believe me?"

"Of course I do."

Celeste was the May half of a financially beneficial marriage, and not only that, she had cleavage. Ralph had a potbelly, no hair on the crown of his head, and two new knees, but I supposed it was possible she spoke the truth.

"Oh, Nell," she wailed. Tears streamed down her cheeks, bringing mascara with them. "I didn't know until now what you must've been going through all these months since Max left you. What am I going to do? I'm not strong, not like you."

"You'll be fine," I said, glancing at my wristwatch. "I'm really sorry, but I've got to go—"

Celeste sniffled and pulled away from the side of the car. "I only thought you'd be interested in knowing about the guy who came round looking for Max yesterday afternoon."

"Guy? What guy?"

"I thought he was Indiana Jones in his khaki shorts and fedora, but he said he was one of Max's college roommates."

I frowned. I'd seen that guy. When I had lunch with Gillian. Jill thought he'd looked familiar. More to the point, she thought he'd been watching us. Now I wondered if she was right.

So, the guy with the hairy legs had been one of Max's roommates. I hadn't known any of his roommates. Max had gone to school back east. "You talked to him?"

"Well, sure. He was pretty interested in your Thunderbird." Celeste nodded at Max's collector's car sitting under a blanket in the extra parking space of my driveway. I'd had to move it out of the garage when the renters moved in. "Besides, he had cute buns, and he was driving a Wrangler. Naturally, I came over and asked if I could help."

"Didn't he tell you his name?" I asked. "Didn't he know that Max is gone?"

She shook her head, then burst into a fresh torrent of tears. "He said to tell Max that he won't stop until he gets the money he's owed." Celeste bit her lip and closed her eyes. Without saying another word, she darted back across the street.

So the guy with hairy legs wasn't just looking for Max. He was looking for money. The same money, I wondered, that was stashed inside a fireproof box?

Eleven

SPEEDING BACK ACROSS town, I decided that Jackson James had some questions to answer. I wondered if Felix's fireproof box of money was somehow connected to Max. I would bet on it. I did not know why Jackson was looking for it. But at least now I suspected that the guy with hairy legs and a fedora—Max's college roommate—was the same one Jackson feared was chasing him. Now he was following me. Because of the money he thought Max owed him?

Jackson had given me his card to call him if any "suspicious-looking characters" showed up, looking for the fireproof box. I had to say, Celeste's guy qualified as a suspicious character.

With questions spinning around in my mind, I pulled into my parking space, sprang out of the car, and ran to the back door of the karate studio. I had left Jackson's card in my in-box, awaiting proper filing in my kitchen office. I would have to call him.

The phone at the other end of the number rang and rang. No pick-up. No voicemail.

I sighed and threw the receiver back in its cradle. I was getting a lot of no answers, and I was fed up with it. Was there a city-wide phone boycott going on, and I hadn't gotten the memo?

That's when I noticed the blinking light, indicating that I had a message. I pressed "play" and listened to Terra chew gum before she gave me a name and an address. "Pearle Pittman," she said, and then explained, "She was friends with that old woman Alice worked for. Mrs. Harris, y'know? They were both birdwatchers."

The address wasn't far from here.

Her house was another Victorian, like Alice's, except its clapboard siding painted with a fresh coat of lavender wouldn't fare as well in a fire. A driveway turned off the street and ran alongside the house to a detached garage in back. I turned into the driveway as a car sped by behind me, whooshing through a puddle left by somebody's lawn sprinkler.

It was a Jeep.

A woman looked up from a flowerbed, where she was deadheading zinnias. "Are you okay, honey? Did that car splash you?"

I turned to the source of the kindly voice, a frail-looking woman under a straw hat. She hunched forward from her mobile garden seat. "Maybe just a little. It's okay."

"Tsk, tsk. It's not okay. Traffic circles and speed bumps don't slow them down." She shook her head and dropped a handful of dead flowers into a bucket at her feet. "I declare, the whole world's afire. What's it going to take? The death of a child playing outside?"

I felt myself go numb. One wrong step, and the Jeep would've hit me. But what bothered me even more was wondering if it was the same Jeep that Celeste had just told me about—a Wrangler. Because that would mean that the guy with the hairy legs had found me and was on my trail again.

"Oh dear, I'm sorry," said the woman. "Silly of me to say such a thing." She rose to a wobbly standing position, holding tightly to the handles of her seat, and then shuffled closer. "I'm Pearle Pittman. I was just about to brew myself some tea. Would you like a cup, dearie?"

"Very much, thank you. I'm Nell Letterly, and I actually came here to see you. I live next door to the house that burned." I took her hand and absorbed the old lady's vitality, flowing through her grip.

She clucked her tongue and shook her head. "Terrible, that."

I followed her to her front door, and she held it open for me to pass through first. The musty smell of antiques greeted me as I stepped onto an oval, hooked rug.

She nodded at a neat row of vintage footwear, all of it the same size and lined up on a smaller, discount-store rug by the door. "You can leave your shoes there." Her head dipped with disapproval at my tennis shoes. "Use a pair of my slippers. They're clean. Washed them myself last week."

"Oh, I don't need slippers, Mrs. Pittman."

"What nonsense." She selected a pair of sensible slip-ons from a box. "And another thing," she said, handing them to me. "Call me Pearle. I've never been married. Never had any inclination, either."

I pulled off my shoes and stepped into the fake fur.

She leaned closer, peering at my T-shirt, and poked a spot on my collarbone. "Honey, that fool sprayed you, didn't he? Somebody's got to stop 'em. You wait right here." She bustled off through one of the doors of the entry hall, and I wondered if she was off to "get" the Jeep. She was back in a flash with a towel.

After dabbing my shoulder with it, she headed through another door, leading the way through a dining room dominated by a dark, oval table with a dozen ladder-back chairs. Matching cabinets held dishes of every color and shape. Above them, a shelf displayed jammed rows of miniature, ceramic birds in various poses. I hurried to catch up.

Pearle disappeared into a sunny kitchen where I blinked from the sudden light. She directed me into one of two chairs at a white table, then struck a match, holding it to the burner of the gas stove like the one Mother had in the 'fifties. She filled a copper kettle, clanked it down onto the burner, and then tapped the glass window above the stove. "Pesky squirrel. Thinks I put birdseed out for him. I saw a tanager yesterday. You like birds, honey?"

I didn't know the difference between a tanager and a sparrow, but I nodded anyway. Pearle didn't appear to notice, as she flew around the kitchen, clinking flowered china cups and filling a plate with home-baked cookies. I felt as if I'd come home.

"The birds will be off to their winter homes soon," she said, pausing to glance out the window. "It's going to be an early winter, you mark my words. Did you know the birds travel thousands of miles? Some of them come up here from way down in South America. And what do they get for their trouble if they don't time things just right? Snow! But they don't let it get them down. They're fighters, and they keep going, no matter what. I always wondered why. What makes them so strong? Why do they risk everything when it would be easier to stay in South America? And now I think I know what it is. It's a change of location. Does them good."

I let her prattle on. I was too busy soaking up the warm vibes in Pearle's kitchen to interrupt her with my questions about Mrs. Harris and her health. More specifically, her death. If I stayed here long enough, I thought the hole in my heart that Max had put there might begin to heal.

"Don't you think so?" Her pause demanded an answer.

"Excuse me?" I felt my cheeks flush from my lack of attention, but she showed no signs of impatience.

"A change of location does a body good, don't you think, honey?"

"I'm sure you're right." That's what I was doing with my life, and look where my mid-life change had taken me.

"Sometimes Elta and I would get on the bus to Denver and go down there to visit my cousin Florence."

"Elta?"

"My friend, Elta Harris. I sure do miss her. She passed on... let's see, it's been two summers now. She didn't have any family, and my cousin Florence didn't mind if I brought her along with me. Give that girl, her companion, a day off every once in a while. Elta always said I should get me a companion, too, but I don't know. I told her 'maybe one day when I get good and old'!" She burst into cackles.

"I'm sorry you lost your friend. Had she been ill a long while?"

"Goodness, no. Healthy and hale, she was. I always did say that when my time comes, I want to go out just the way she did. Went to bed one night and never woke up. What did you want to see me about, dearie?"

Mrs. Harris had probably died of a heart attack in her sleep, I told myself, and not because Alice had added anything to her warm milk for bedtime. "Mrs. Harris's companion is my friend, and I wondered what you think about her inheriting your friend's house."

"Well, there's not much to think, now is there? Elta didn't have anyone else to leave it to. Not like me, with Florence and her folks. 'Course, I can't always count on the little neighbor boy to feed my birds when I'm gone. But I declare, that girl of Elta's lifted her heart. It's a pity, though, what she did to Elta's house, turning it into a store. Although, those little candies she set out for her customers were to die for. I must get her recipe. And then the store nearly burned down, I hear tell. Still, I guess it was a change of scenery for both of them, and that's never a bad thing. Even though Florence is not far away, every time when I come back home after visiting her, nothing seems as bad as I thought it was before."

I needed to start paying attention, because she was talking to me, even in her roundabout manner. As if this wise old woman intuitively understood my situation.

And because of her prattle, I knew that I had to rely on my intuition, too.

Twelve

NO SOONER HAD I returned to my filing in the kitchen office of the studio than pounding came from the front door. The sound straightened my spine. People didn't usually come round here before the studio opened in the late afternoons (except Saturdays). And except for the police.

Alice must've finally come back.

It had to be Alice. I fairly skipped through the studio, racing to the front door, pulled it open, and... It wasn't Alice.

A man grinned at me through a wooly beard and from under an orange baseball cap that sported the local football logo with the reminder of their crush ability. He thrust his hand at me. Either it was the offer of a handshake, or it was the sloppiest ridge hand strike in the history of martial arts. "The name's Steele," he said. "Steele Dickensen."

I decided it was a handshake and accepted his gesture, but he dropped my hand before he'd barely shaken it. "Got a minute?" He wore stiff cowboy boots, expensive jeans, and a T-shirt advertising a microbrew.

The man was in a rush, I decided. Fortunately, I wasn't. I responded with a flick of my wrist to glance at my sports watch.

"I won't keep you long. I'm a reporter for the *Chronicle*, the weekly newspaper. It's justifiably called a 'rag,' but the stories are fun." He eyed me carefully, as if that would change my mind about how busy I was.

My first inclination, considering my experience with reporters these past nine months since Max disappeared, was to shut the door in the journalist's face, but then I spied the carpet cleaner sitting in a corner of the porch, behind the glider. My dad must've dropped it off for me while I was out. I remembered Hennesey's warnings not to talk to any reporters, but I wanted the carpet cleaner even more. I stepped toward it and said, "What can I do for you, Mr. Dickensen?"

"Please. Call me Steele. I'm following up on the fire you had next door." He nodded in the direction of Alice's burned house. "That was my photo spread you saw in yesterday's paper. All the dailies used it, plus the AP."

Pausing, I folded my arms against my chest. "You make it sound as if the neighborhood planned it for their entertainment."

"But it *did* entertain the neighbors, didn't it? It was a lot of excitement for them night before last."

I suppressed a shudder and narrowed my eyes at him. "Tragedy is hardly entertaining. Now, if you don't mind, I have a busy schedule." I made a move to haul the carpet cleaner inside.

"Yes, I can see that." His gaze swept up and down my body, taking in the running shorts and this year's *Bolder Boulder* T-shirt. "Please. I won't keep you long."

Being a sucker for the p-word, I set down the carpet cleaner and leaned against the doorframe, waiting for him to go on. But I didn't invite him in.

He grinned and said, "I understand she was your friend."

"And still is."

"Some of your other neighbors have hinted that she had

some financial difficulties that insurance money is going to solve nicely for her."

"They're mistaken."

One of his shaggy eyebrows arched up. "You're sure?"

"Of course I'm sure! I know Alice. You said so yourself."

He stroked his scraggly beard. "I wonder. How well can you really know a person in only five months?"

"Well enough." My blood ran cold. This wasn't supposed to be about me. But if he knew Alice had been my friend for precisely five months, then he knew I'd lived here that long. I wondered what else he knew. The circumstances of my move had to do with Max. Was that what the reporter was driving at?

Hennesey had tried to warn me.

"Then, maybe you can tell me about Alice's affair with the artist who was living with her. Felix Todd."

"He rented studio space from her, that's all."

"Are you sure that was all?"

No, I wasn't sure, but I wasn't going to tell him that. I glared at him. "What are you driving at?"

"The relationship may have been, shall we say, rocky."

"I wouldn't know about that."

"Ah! Then you don't know her after all."

I sighed. "I'm sorry, I can't help you." I pulled away from the doorframe. He could forget it.

"Because there's something embarrassing to learn about her?"

"Because I have no comment." I glared at him and reached for the door handle.

"If you won't talk about her, then I'd like to ask you a few questions about the string of murders that seem to have crossed your path recently." He pulled a tattered notebook and chewed stub of a pencil from his hip pocket and returned my gaze with an equally intent one of his own. Probably watching for signs of fluster. He found none, despite my confusion about the way he'd made the word plural.

"String?"

"Enrique Valencia," he read from his notebook.

"Would that be Rick Valencia?" My unfortunate predecessor. "I never knew him."

Dickensen frowned. "He'd been the head instructor here at your *dojo* for two years before he met his untimely end. Before *you* arrived on the scene."

"Then you already know as much about him as I do."

He laughed. "Oh, I have a few facts about him, that's all." He waited, with pencil poised, as if giving me the opportunity to add to his short list of facts.

"Very impressive," I said, "but all that was five months ago. Old news."

He laughed again. "Oh, no. That story's not done yet. It's a big story, and they're keeping a tight lid on it, on account of legalization. But I intend to take the lid off."

I felt my skin crawl. What did marijuana have to do with those murders? They happened when I first moved into the karate studio. I'd had to earn my living after Max left... I couldn't imagine that the scandal of his disappearance actually had anything to do with the legalization of marijuana.

I was finished, but Steele Dickensen wasn't ready to go yet. He read off another name from his notebook. "Francesca Denton."

Something tightened in my chest. "Who?"

"Young woman who died after an unfortunate fall from the Flatirons." He looked up from his notes and sobered, waiting for this to refresh my memory.

My veins tightened, and he went on. "She was a student here in this studio, I'm told."

Now the tightening turned to a stranglehold. Even so, I kept my voice level. "I never knew her, either. She was a student here before my time as instructor."

That gave him something to think about, and he bought time by flipping through the pages of his notebook. "Guess she hadn't taken lessons long enough to learn much about defending herself."

"Even the most experienced martial artists can become victims," I said, "as my predecessor's unfortunate death should've indicated."

His gaze rolled slowly off my face and turned uphill to the charred remainders of Alice's shop. "And now we have the death of Felix Todd. World-renowned western landscape artist. But you probably didn't know him, either."

My skin prickled. Lightheaded, I swayed and reached out to steady myself against the door. "How'd *you* find out his identity? The police aren't giving out that information yet."

Dickensen blinked at me and grinned. "Of course they aren't. But thanks for confirming."

My gut twisted inside, falling for his tricks. "Look, what are you getting at? You think I have some sort of connection to those deaths?"

"Maybe you understand more than you think," he continued, as if that explained everything.

I remembered my lessons from Master Hwang and stood

straight, short, and impassive, despite the thumping that was running through my veins, resounding in my ears. "No, I believe you've made a mistake. I can't help you."

"Think again."

When I wouldn't answer, he annoyed me some more. "I believe *you're* the connection that'll make this story go off like a bomb. Don't you think it's curious, Mrs. Gannon, that *you*, of all people, work in a place where those victims were associated?"

I felt my ram-rod straight back go even stiffer. The black mass of curls around his mouth parted again. He was waiting for me to trip up now that he'd spoken the name I never used, informing me that he'd done his research. He knew all about Max. And he knew exactly who I was.

But how had he known to find me *here*?

"What I think is curious, Mr. Dickensen, is where you get your information."

He shrugged. "Hey, I'm a journalist. It's what I do. I listen to the police scanner and ask lots of questions. Take, for instance, the car accident yesterday in the alley a couple blocks up from here. Silver Honda. You know anything about that?"

"Jackson?" Jackson James couldn't leave here fast enough the day before in his silver car. Shortly before that accident in the alley. Dad must've heard about it, too, on the scanner. "That was *Jack*?"

"See what I mean? Isn't it curious how *you* seem to be the point in common between all of these so-called accidents?"

"What happened?"

"He lost control of his vehicle. Looks like the tire went flat. Maybe even slashed. Hit a trashcan."

"Is he...? How is he?" I recalled the brief article I'd read in the morning newspaper. *Man Found Dead on the Hill...*

"Didn't make it."

"Oh no!" My hand flew up to cover my mouth. Jackson had been so alive just a short while before that. Afraid of something... Afraid of suspicious characters chasing him for Felix's fireproof box of money. Maybe the guy in the fedora had caught up with him.

The reporter went on. "This didn't make it into the paper, so this is just between you and me, see? He didn't die due to injuries sustained in the crash. He died from a knife wound."

I gasped. "But... He was just *here*. He was on his way home."

Dickensen poised his pencil over his notebook. "What'd he say to you?"

"Nothing," I said, perhaps a bit too hastily. "Nothing important."

The reporter grunted and flipped the pages of his notepad. He found a business card tucked between the pages and handed it to me. "Once you think about it some more, and give yourself a chance to remember something that will shed light on these cases, give me a call."

"There's nothing to remember." I crossed my fingers with my lie. "And now, I have a lot of work to do, so I must ask you to leave." I wouldn't back down, and I hoped I wouldn't have to throw him off the premises. He must've weighed twice as much as I did.

"Okay, okay," he said, taking my tone of voice seriously. He stuffed his notebook back into his pocket and clomped down the porch steps. "But I'll be back."

I'm sure you will, I thought, clutching his card tight between my fingers and fighting the tremor in my knees. I waited until he disappeared down the street before lugging the carpet cleaner inside and clicking the door locked.

Thirteen

DOUBTS GNAWED AT the back of my mind the rest of the day, as I ran the carpet cleaner across the buckling folds of the workout floor. The reporter had seemed convincing, although hard to believe. Was it true that Jackson was really dead?

I'd seen the flashing lights of the police cars.

Jackson had been so full of life, just a short while before that. Then he'd seen *me*, and...

Someone had stabbed him to death, according to the reporter.

Because, the reporter had insinuated, I was a magnet for crime. Was that true? If so, then my friend and neighbor's house had deliberately been torched because of *me*. With Felix, trapped inside.

Maybe it wasn't me. More likely, it was because of the sale of unlicensed edibles that Robinette arranged. Or maybe it was because I could identify the cabin that Felix had painted in his depiction of a marijuana field. Mountain High, indeed.

I worked straight through dinner. Thankfully, Gillian treated Terra to dinner after band camp.

And when I was finally done with the carpets, I'm not sure why—maybe I forgot to tell the car where I was supposed to go. Or maybe I was still too rattled from the reporter's information.

Or maybe I just wasn't ready to face Terra and Gillian yet, who knew? Anyway, I ended up back on my old street, in the old neighborhood once again. The suburbs north of town.

I parked several houses away from mine. I wouldn't want to be considered a prowler at my own house, after all. How embarrassing that would be. I would just sit here a few moments, breathing deeply, pondering the loss of my old life. For a fraction of a second, I wondered if it was possible to go backwards in time and recover what Max and I'd once had.

The excuse I gave myself for coming here was that I was going to need a lawyer soon. Somehow I sensed that. After all, my divorce loomed imminently. And Celeste's husband was a lawyer.

I unlocked the car door and climbed out. A rude wind slapped me in the face, tousled my hair, and sent a shiver down my spine. After dark, the air cooled off fast, even in August.

I'd never noticed before how dark it was at this post-dinner hour of the evening. Or maybe it only seemed darker to me now. The neighborhood association had always had problems with the streetlights we'd privately installed. More often than not, they didn't work. Now the lights were out, and the street lay under the shroud of night.

The scent of some neighbor's late dinner of grilled steak reached me via their vent and the gusts of wind. It could be coming from Celeste's house where a romantic, candle-lit, fashionably late dinner was in progress. I was about to find out. I marched across the cul-de-sac and up to Celeste and Ralph's front door. The porch light wasn't on, but I rang the bell anyway.

After an uncomfortably long wait, the front door opened and Celeste appeared. Her penciled eyebrows contorted, and tears streaked her cheeks.

"Oh, Nell!" she cried, sniffling, still holding the door semi-shut.

"Maybe I should come back another time?"

"Noooo," she wailed, pulling the door open and stepping aside for me to enter.

Cautiously, I slid past the door, then stood in the entryway, staring at Celeste. She was dressed in something silky, sexy, and black.

"Er, I'm interrupting," I said, creeping back toward the threshold.

"Not anymore." Celeste sobbed and grabbed me by the wrist. "It didn't work out." She released my wrist to cover her face with her hands and burst into a torrent of fresh tears.

"Oh, Celeste," I murmured, staring longingly at the door. "I have to go."

"You can't leave me, too! I don't want to be alone at a time like this. God, I need a drink." Celeste flounced into the living room, a softly lit room in tans and beiges.

I shut the door and followed her past a row of columns that separated the entry from the living room. Celeste stood at a marble-topped bar, where she poured something clear from what looked like a pregnant bottle containing a pear. She turned and handed me a crystal thimble on a stem.

"Cheers," she said, then upended hers and poured another.

"Likewise." I lifted my miniature glass, but toxic fumes stopped me before the drink hit my lips. "What is this stuff?"

"Like Grappa, only better. Go on, try it. You'll like it."

I tried again, and this time barely wet my throat. I gasped. If fire were liquid, this was it.

"Good, isn't it?" she said, pouring her third glass. "I brought it back myself from my last trip to Geneva."

"Cheeesssssus," I finally hissed.

"Let's sit down." Carrying the bottle of fire, Celeste led me to the overstuffed sofa and plopped down onto it.

"You want to tell me about it?" I asked, as a means of offering her an opening.

"I can't." She swallowed another thimble-full, then reached for the bottle on the glass-topped coffee table.

I sniffed my fumes again. My eyes started to water. "What did Ralph say when he left?"

"I can't talk about it."

I sighed. This was going to be a long night. Then again, I thought, watching her pour and drink, maybe not so long. "Can you tell me where he went?"

"What the hell do I care where he went?"

"What if someone is looking for him?" *Someone like me.* I remembered my purpose.

She giggled. "That's their problem, isn't it?"

"It may be important. Ralph's a lawyer, after all."

"Maybe he went to the condo." Then a spasm overcame her, and she dropped her glass on the sofa and shuddered with sobs. "Who will get the condo if we divorce? I don't want a divorce! I love him! I truly do!"

I found a stack of cocktail napkins in the bar, grabbed a handful and dabbed at the spill on the velour fabric of the sofa.

"You've got to believe me, Nell!"

"I do, honey."

"You're too kind," she said. "How can I repay you?"

"It's not—"

"I know!" she said, brightening, not paying a bit of attention to her glass as I clinked it down on the table. "You can use my condo!"

"Thanks, but—"

"I insist!" Her eyes blazed at me.

I wondered why everyone was trying to get me into the mountains. First Jackson, now Celeste. But she probably wouldn't remember in the morning. Her mind flitted elsewhere.

"You don't believe me, do you?" she said. "You're just saying that you do, but you don't, not really. No one believes that I really love him. Everyone thinks I just married him for his money because he's so much older than me."

She certainly sounded earnest.

"Did you know I've been married before?" she continued, stifling a yawn. "It was a mistake. I was too young. So was he. Not Ralphie, though. Ralph is my stabilizing influence. Oh, what have I done? What am I going to do now?"

"You'll manage," I mumbled.

"How? How? Oh, Nell, you're so strong, and I'm not."

"That's nonsense."

"How'd you get so strong? Is it that karate thing you do? Maybe you're right and it's better to be strong than feminine, since men are just going to leave you anyway."

"Sure, Celeste. Whatever you say."

"Look what happened to you. And now to me. I guess I deserve it, though, don't I?" She fluffed her hair and ran her hand along the lacy front of her top. "Ralph called me a slut. Nell, do you think I'm a slut?"

"No, of course not."

"Yes, you do." Another yawn.

There was no arguing with her under the forces of Grappa. "Look, why don't you go to bed now, and I'll just be leaving—"

"No, stay! I can't stand to be alone!"

"I *can't* stay, and you'll be fine. But I'll help you into bed before I go. Come on." I pulled her up by one of her anemic arms and steadied her on her feet. Then I guided her to the stairs, where she leaned on me more than the banister.

I'd never been in her bedroom before, and it didn't surprise me to see a leopard-skin throw across a giant-sized bed dominating the room. I guided her to the bed and gave her a little push.

"Good night," I said, tiptoeing to the door.

"By th' way. I saw Max."

"You *what*?" Goosebumps tickled the back of my neck, and I froze with my hand on the doorjamb.

"I'm sure it was him."

"Max was *here*?"

"Mmmm... With the blondes."

"Blondes?"

"Mm-hmmm. One...on each arm."

Silence.

"Celeste?"

Her jaw had fallen open, and she was snoring softly. I'd waited too long. For about a millisecond, I was torn between shaking her awake and making my escape. I chose the easy way.

* * * * *

I did not know how long I stood there on Celeste's doorstep, numb in the night.

Max! Here. In town.

The safe world that I'd begun building for myself just imploded.

Max!

Frankly, I didn't feel any stirrings of jealousy regarding the blondes. Or even if that report was true. Celeste wasn't exactly a reliable witness. She was just a nosy neighbor, who sometimes expanded her reports into fantasies, colored by Grappa.

Truth was, I was over Max, and that was good to know for sure. What upset me even more than his flagrant infidelity was the fact that he'd come back. If, in fact, that was a fact.

I didn't believe it.

If he truly wanted to come back, maybe to his old job, he would make a big splash of it. He would have to do it that way, after the scandal of his disappearance. He wouldn't just quietly return.

Surely, he didn't expect to reconcile with *me*. The blonde on each arm told me that much. Then, why would he sneak around? To sign the divorce papers? Doubtful. To kidnap Terra? Even less likely. Honestly, he'd never cared much about being a parent. To collect Felix's fireproof box of money? I didn't think it would be worth his time and effort for a few hundred bucks. And how likely was it that he'd even known about the cash through a casual contact at the cooking school?

No, it was more likely he'd returned for the sadistic pleasure of seeking revenge against me. After all, I'd become the b-lady and had stood up to him. Still, I couldn't see him scratching the b-word into the side of my car. Maybe he'd started the fire at Alice's, intending it to be for me, to show me his prowess, but he'd goofed and torched the wrong house. That, I could believe.

Or maybe he'd come back because of some deal he couldn't

miss out on. Maybe something to do with Jackson. And the box of money. After all, Jackson had been asking a lot of questions about Max, questions that had seemingly come out of left field. *Maybe not so far left.*

The rattling sound of an engine brought me out of my stupor. A car was making its way slowly up the hill. Already I could see its headlights bouncing off the pavement as it plowed up the hill toward the spot where I stood.

Without thinking, I stepped away from Celeste's front door and crouched behind a juniper.

Hiding there like a criminal, I breathed in the pungent perfume of a branch scratching my nose. What on earth was I doing? But it was too late now to creep out of my hiding place without startling whichever former neighbor who was probably returning home. The headlights coming my way were large, round circles, closer together than the standard car's.

It was a Jeep. Maybe even a Wrangler.

The Jeep slowed, stopping on the other side of my juniper. The driver's door opened, and a tall man in a fedora and shorts climbed out. He probably had hairy legs, although it was too dark for me to see that well.

He helped a large dog out of the Jeep and snapped a leash on the animal. The dog turned immediately toward the direction of my hiding place, planted its hind legs, and started to bark. The dog's owner murmured something and tugged at the leash.

Definitely a man's stride, I thought, watching them as they made their way toward my house. Renters lived there now. Not me.

The dog stopped at my yard and sniffed the flowerbed where my renter had planted petunias. Then it lifted its leg to leave its mark. Another male.

Circling in my flowerbed, he apparently became interested in leaving me another present. His guardian's attention was focused on my house, instead of what his dog was doing to my property. No lights shone from the windows, a message that the renters had gone out for the evening, leaving the place unguarded.

The dog's guardian reached into his pocket and pulled out a plastic newspaper wrapper along with a small notepad. He must've had one of those leashes that expand a long way, for he left the dog squatting in the flower bed while he sauntered up the driveway to where Max's Thunderbird sat in one corner under a car blanket. He lifted one end of its protective cover, revealing the collector's license plate, and scribbled a note. Then the man circled around to the driver's side of the Thunderbird. Again he lifted the cover. This time he pulled out of his pocket a small flashlight, which he shone into the interior of the car.

The dog barked, tentatively at first, then with more persistence. The man quickly dropped the canvas cover, pocketed his flash and notepad, and surveyed the dark surroundings. He hurried back to the dog's side and bent over him, using the plastic wrapper as a glove. The dog continued to bark.

Tying up the plastic bag, the tall man pulled at the leash and dragged the animal, whose barking grew more intense, away from my flowerbed. Next door, the Braunsteins' porch light turned on. The man pulled the bill of his fedora down lower over his brow and strode briskly toward the Jeep.

The dog pumped his legs to keep up, until the man opened the passenger's door of the Jeep. The dog balked, pricked up his ears and whimpered, staring straight at me.

The man mumbled something and shoved the animal up onto the seat. He threw the plastic bag in, shut the dog's door, and glanced around once more. Hurrying to the driver's side, he climbed in and switched on the lights. As he rolled away, I read the license plates: "XTRMN8."

Fourteen

I STOOD THERE staring at the Exterminator's tags for what seemed like forever, pondering what he had been looking for.

Braunstein turned off his porch lights, snapping me out of my daze. I darted down the sidewalk toward my car. Breathless, I reached the Ghia with keys in hand, sprang inside and rumbled down the street after the Jeep. Then it occurred to me that I didn't know what I would do with him if I caught him. That was enough of a doubt to make my foot slide off the accelerator.

I could hear Master Hwang's chiding tongue in my head. *Okay*, I told him, and I kept going.

But at the first intersection I lost the Jeep. He'd vanished down one of those silent, dark streets, slipping into the shadows, maybe turning the tables and watching me at that very moment. I killed the engine and unrolled the window. No distant rumble of a car disturbed the night. I started up the car again and cruised around several blocks, searching driveways for Jeeps.

Nothing.

Finally I gave up. Good thing the Ghia knew its way across town. I drove mechanically, in a daze.

Max! Back in town.

And already with two blondes. That's what Celeste had said. Maybe it was the Grappa speaking for her. But whether

her perception had been confused or not, the truth was, two blondes weren't so hard to believe of Max.

When I surfaced from my daze, I was sitting safely inside my car, parked on the quiet side street in front of Gillian's townhouse. I didn't know how long I had been sitting there.

The man from the Jeep—Max's college roommate—had been interested in the Thunderbird's license number, and then something in the front seat—maybe the registration in the glove compartment. But his dog had interrupted. I could think of only one reason for his interest—he'd been confirming that the vehicle was, indeed, Max's cherished collector's car. That car was the one thing Max would've regretted leaving behind. Perhaps he'd hired his old school chum, the guy in the Jeep, the guy with hairy legs, to steal the car for him.

Maybe Celeste really had seen Max.

I sighed and climbed out of the car.

Penelope, the Golden Retriever, pushed in front of Gillian to greet me at her door. The dog click-clacked down the wood floor of the hall, leading the way to the family room at the back of the townhouse. Gillian was in the middle of loading the dishwasher as Terra thumbed her currently favorite game on her cell phone. She'd earned the phone herself, cleaning toilets at the karate studio three times per week. That made her officially on Arlo Callahan's payroll. I couldn't complain.

Well, actually I could. I was the b-lady, after all. But it wasn't a school night, not for a couple more weeks, so I gave her a break. I deposited a kiss on the crown of her head, and she released one thumb to quickly wave her hand at me, as if shooing away a pesky bee.

"Where have you been?" Gillian said from the other side of

the breakfast bar that divided the kitchen from the family room.

"Working." My cheeks flamed.

"It sure took you a long while, just to do that little bitty carpet over there."

"Uh-huh."

"You could've laid an entire new carpet in the same amount of time it took you to clean it."

"Probably." Gillian wouldn't have a clue about laying carpets.

Gillian's face flushed, the way it did when she'd made a new conquest and was busting inside to gloat about it. "You must be starving. We have leftover take-out Thai, if you want some for dinner."

"Sounds good." I crossed my fingers with my lie. My agreeable nature was for their benefit, in case either of them was actually listening to me. The truth was, I was suspicious of any food with a name I couldn't pronounce. I couldn't help myself. I was my father's daughter.

Gillian heated up a plate of what looked like noodles (fancy that!) in the microwave and plopped it down on the breakfast bar. "Want a beer to go with?" she said, reaching into the fridge.

"Uh, sure." I hated beer, but I knew that Gillian didn't keep pitchers of iced tea around here. "So, what's up? Did something happen with that Condo character? You were going to check out his development plans, so I imagine by now you have a date with him. Is that what you're so bubbly about?"

"Oh, Nell, don't be silly." She popped the pop-top on the can and scooted it before me. "It's not a *date*, for goodness sake. He's old enough to be my father. I'm just helping you out, that's all."

Right. A rich father, I thought. Money always spoke to Gillian.

"Did you see him?" I asked.

"Not yet. I have an appointment with him day after tomorrow. He's going to show me one of his projects. He's looking for an investor, and I told his assistant that I represent the family back east, and we're looking for real estate investments. That part is true, you know."

"Are you really going to commit the family money to Jimmie Condo?"

She shrugged. "It depends on what he offers. I'm always open to a good deal. But that won't interest you. What *will* interest you is what's hanging on the wall in his office."

I lifted an eyebrow.

"That's right. It's called 'Mountain High'." Her grin reached ear to ear. "Jimmie Condo is our secret art collector! Don't you love it?"

I wasn't sure. "Does this have something to do with his interest in Alice's property?"

"Oh, Nell, you're always so suspicious."

I grimaced and took a long swallow of beer.

"Okay, now you give," she said. "What's the latest scoop on our mystery?"

Terra looked up from her game.

Jackson was dead. I wasn't emotionally ready to tell them that news yet, so I said instead, "I still have no idea where Alice is."

"Give her time." Gillian wiped her hands on a dishtowel and joined me at the breakfast bar with a glass of something tawny red, looking like port. "It was a tragic accident, and Alice will need to heal. It's too soon to jump to any conclusions."

"I bet she's gone into hiding," Terra said, "because she's afraid of getting caught."

Gillian perked up. "For what? For being charged with murder?"

"Maybe," Terra said. "Or maybe she's hiding some*thing*."

A fireproof box filled with money came to mind. The box someone had killed Jackson for. He'd died from a *knife* wound, the journalist had said, egging me on, because that's how my predecessor had also died.

Then I remembered that Dominic had lost a knife. Had someone with access to his cooking school picked it up?

"Then," Gillian said, swirling her glass of port, "you think Alice killed Felix?"

"Hey, you two," I said. "Stop it. That's enough. Alice did no such thing."

"But Mom," Terra said, "what if she had a big fight with Felix and wanted to get rid of him?"

Gillian turned to me. "*Did* she have a quarrel with him?"

I sighed. "His ex-wife thinks so, but that doesn't mean Alice set her own house on fire. It's just not logical. I think it's more likely that she's afraid of some arsonist who meant for her to become the victim. And she's gone away because she doesn't want to drag me—us—into it, too."

"Sometimes arguments can get out of hand," Gillian said. "She wouldn't have meant to do it."

"Yeah, Mom, and then a fire would cover her tracks."

I shook my head. "It makes no sense. Alice lost her house in that fire and everything in it. Why would she do that deliberately to herself?"

Terra shrugged. "Well, you're the one who wanted me to find out on the internet about what went down in California."

My skin prickled. "And you found something?"

"The archives from the local newspaper where she supposedly came from reported about an Alice Brightall who—"

"Brightall?" I snapped. "As in an anagram for Albright?"

"You want to hear what I found, or not?" Terra said.

"Sorry. Go on."

"Well, there was this fire, see? And her boyfriend died in it."

"The abusive one?"

"How would I know? The article didn't say that. All it said was that she was eventually acquitted of manslaughter charges."

"Bottom line, Nell," Gillian said. "The ex-boyfriend from California is dead, so we can eliminate him as a suspect for arson here."

"Then who—?" I broke off, wagging my head in self-pity. If only they understood. If only *I* understood.

Gillian set down her port and used both hands to explain. "Maybe the California boyfriend had a friend who blames Alice for his death. And maybe he's seeking revenge against her."

"How would we know where to find him?"

"I dunno," Gillian said. "You're the sleuth. You tell us."

"I don't think it's anyone from California."

"How do you know that?" Terra said.

"Because abusive boyfriends are just plain stupid," I said, winging it. Truth was, I didn't know. I was making it up as I went. "They're too stupid to have cunning friends who are smart enough to seek revenge. And anyway, Alice was starting over when she came here. She even has a new identity here. She changed her name. The abusive boyfriend can never hurt her again. So she has no reason to hide from him, right?"

I thought back to my conversation with Alice over iced tea when she'd first told me about the abusive boyfriend. Because she hadn't exactly said he was *dead,* I assumed he was alive. My poor friend. She must've been too traumatized, even though she'd been acquitted of any responsibility in that fire. The coincidence of her having gone through two fires in two states hung like a pall over my plate of noodles.

That, and Jackson.

Terra sighed and went back to her game.

Gillian swallowed the last of her port and poured another. She was a budding Celeste. "I told you it wasn't safe to live over there in *That Place.* But you wouldn't listen. You never do."

I fell silent, lost in my own thoughts as I wrestled with slippery noodles.

"Talk to me, Nell. What are you thinking?"

I munched slowly. "I have an idea. If it's truly a case of arson, and not just a dumb accident because Felix was absent-minded and threw turpentine onto his stove, or something stupid like that, then the arsonist was most likely in the crowd of rubber neckers the night of the fire. Arsonists are drawn to fires—especially to the ones they set."

"Where do you come up with this stuff? Sometimes you make my head hurt." Gillian sipped her port.

I ignored that. "So, who was there that night?"

"Lots of people. Did you take roll call?"

I held up my hand and ticked off my index finger as my first point. "*Creations by Erica.* That woman has enough anger in her to ignite anything on fire if she just walks past. And did you

155

see that graffiti on my car?"

"You think she did that?"

"Uh-huh."

"But you can't know for sure she's the one."

"Who else?" Of course there was Max, I thought. He always made a good suspect. But I bit my tongue to keep from divulging his presence in town. Max would have to contact his daughter and his half-sister himself. And if he didn't, then I wasn't going to be the one to hurt Terra and Gillian by letting them know that he was in town and didn't care enough to at least call up and say hello.

"You're right," Gillian said. "She was angry enough at Alice to want to hurt her business. Maybe she also wanted to pay her back for stealing her husband."

"Eliminating all possibility forever of child support?"

"Maybe Felix is worth more dead," Terra said without looking up from her game. "Won't the kid end up getting the money from Felix's paintings?"

"Time for you to be in bed, young lady," I said.

"You're no fun." Terra slowly gathered up her things, lingering every step of the way.

"But she has a point, Nell," Gillian said. "Felix's paintings have gone way up in value now, with all the notoriety. And the fire reduced his inventory, making the rest of the collection much more valuable."

"Are you suggesting that someone burned him out to make his other paintings that much more valuable?"

"Hey, we're just throwing out ideas," Gillian said. "For instance, do you really believe Alice when she said she was at the movies? How do you know for sure that's where she was?

Did you ask her what she'd seen?"

I frowned. Actually, Alice had been evasive when I'd asked her about the movie.

"Maybe she had a hot date," Gillian went on, "and doesn't want to talk about it. And as long as we're throwing out ideas, here's another one for you: what about Jackson? He has a new girlfriend, and he doesn't want to talk about her, either."

"Duh," Terra said, unearthing a library book from under a cushion.

"Off with you," I said, pointing to the stairs in the hall. "March."

Terra stomped out of the room.

"Robinette," Gillian said, ticking off two fingers. "That must be his new girlfriend. She was there, and you said she was acting overly weird."

I shook my head. "Robinette is young enough to be Jackson's daughter." She *was* Dominic's daughter.

"Which would be why he doesn't want to talk about her. Wake up, Nell. It can happen."

That was just the point. I was out of touch. And anyway, I wanted to distract her from the subject of Jackson. Let her find out about his death when his identity was finally released to the public. Any day now.

I slid off the barstool and crossed the room to the coat closet, where I'd hung my mystery book bag on the doorknob. Rummaging inside, I found the can that I'd picked up from Alice's house, then stowed in the Ghia's glove compartment, transferred now to my bag.

"Here, what do you make of this?" I carried it back to Gillian and pulled off the lid.

She crooked her fingers like tweezers and carefully plucked out the glass pieces, then fitted them together like a puzzle. The kitchen light sparkled through the orange and pink swirls.

"It's a broken pipe!" Gillian said. "See?" Her fingers held up two of the curved pieces. "It's hand-blown glass for smoking marijuana. Where'd you get this?"

"Alice's house," I said, feeling suddenly ten times heavier. The weight of doom dragged at my knees and my gut. "Alice used to blow glass in California. She wanted to take it up again here."

"Looks like she did."

What it looked like to me was that the reports of gossip I'd been hearing must be correct. Alice's craft shoppe was more than just a gallery. And it sold more than just crafts. Alice must know about Robinette's marijuana sales. What I didn't understand was why Alice hadn't ever gotten a license to sell it, if selling the stuff was what she'd wanted to do.

And why Jackson was dead because of all this.

Fifteen

THE NEXT MORNING dawned cloudy, which was unusual for a Colorado morning. Summer storms didn't usually hit us until afternoon, and then they were swift and brief.

Shortly after Terra left for band camp, Gillian burst in on me in the middle of my morning stretching and strengthening exercises. "Oh, Nell! The university just phoned. The police are there, in Max's office, someone named Hennesey? And he wants us there."

My heart skipped a beat. "Us?"

"Well, you, actually."

"But why? Why are city police at the university?"

"Beats me. I'm just giving you the message."

"And anyway, hasn't Max's office been assigned to someone else by now?"

"Not yet. It's going to be reallocated to a visiting prof who will be arriving in town soon."

"Hasn't someone boxed up everything of Max's by now?"

She narrowed her eyes at me, then turned on the heels of her furry, pink slippers and stormed out of the guestroom. "I've been doing it. I thought it would upset you too much if you handled it." She slammed the door behind her.

I followed her out into the hall. "Really, you have? I didn't

159

know. Thanks for that."

She nodded. "I'm leaving in ten minutes if you want a ride. I'm stopping for my latte, and I can't be late. I have an appointment with my advisor."

I knew better than to interfere with Gillian and her morning latte.

Twenty minutes later, Gillian eased her Audi into traffic as our twin paper cups released coffee aroma. I lifted the lid of my cup, slurped the steaming froth, and eyed the sky. The clouds had lowered even more, threatening to smother us.

"I haven't packed up everything yet," Gillian said. "There's lots to go through. His research files."

"He'd want you to have all that, Jill."

"He's not dead." She whipped her head around and gave me the evil eye.

"No, of course not," I agreed, glancing at the traffic to encourage her gaze back onto the road.

Her attention thankfully returned to her driving, although she kept chattering. "He'll be back. The division is fighting to keep that space for when he does. The entire school is tight on space, you see, so the division didn't want to lose it. They couldn't touch it the semester he disappeared, and it's only been one semester since. Not counting summer. Some graduate students have been using it as temporary overflow until the new visiting prof arrives. Next week, I believe."

I crammed my cup back into its holder and spilled a trace of coffee on the lacquered finish. "Wait a minute. Are you telling me that the department just let anyone use Max's office with all his stuff still in it?"

"It's called a division, not a department."

"Okay, okay, but I don't understand. I didn't think they'd let students use a faculty office, not without supervision."

"Professor James took complete responsibility. Didn't you know that?"

Jackson was dead, and I hadn't told Gillian yet. "Um, no. They might've at least asked permission."

Gillian's voice lowered. "I told them it would be okay. It's being used for some work study projects, I think."

"Oh." I exhaled sharply and reached into my book bag for a tissue to wipe up my coffee dribble.

"With Max gone indefinitely," Gillian continued as we inched up the long hill toward the university, "you can't expect the school to tie up his space forever."

"I guess not. But what's the police interest in all this? Why are they there? Why do they want *me* there now? Has something been stolen?" I wondered if this had anything to do with Jackson's death. How did one die of a knife injury while driving?

She took her eyes off traffic and aimed those jade slits at me. "Your police friends aren't real talkative."

"They're not my friends."

She whispered, "Jerk," through gritted teeth at a beater that cut her off.

I'd been meaning over the past few months to stop by and poke my nose into Max's affairs at his work—er, I meant, check out the office space he'd left behind—but time had managed to slip away, as it had a way of doing. The task was so low on my list of priorities that I'd forgotten.

We stopped and waited while a city bus emptied its cargo at a bus stop, and then barged back into the flow of traffic. That's

161

how I felt—empty, awkward, and pushy.

"What aren't the police telling us?" I said. "Why aren't they talking to us?"

"I suspect the way you've been so nosy has complicated things. Why would the police volunteer information to us now?"

I sighed. Girl sleuth, at work again. "It can't be about something stolen. Who would want to steal any research data lying around after all this time?"

"You said it yourself last night, Nell. It's all about competition. Erica and Alice were highly competitive, even in the craft industry. Take, for example, Max and Professor James's professional rivalry."

And now Jackson was dead and Max was back in town.

* * * * *

I wasn't prepared for the overwhelming feelings of loss that bowled me over, just seeing the sprawling building where Max used to work. Seeing his building now made me realize that I hadn't moved as far forward with my life as I'd thought. I still had to find closure with the past.

Gillian inserted a faculty parking pass into the gate—somehow she'd managed to procure one. The bar flipped up, and she wheeled into a prized parking spot. She darted off to her appointment while I climbed the stairs to the top floor.

Max had complained for years about the size of his office on the top floor of the Business School. When Gillian came to town two years ago, she felt sorry for him and used her artistic talents to convert the small, disorganized hovel into a cozy nest. She'd even tucked a miniature lamp on one of the bookshelves flanking the door, and placed a calming waterfall in a bowl on his desk.

What she hadn't been able to get rid of was his collection of masks from different countries. They glowered at visitors from their position on the wall behind the desk. Max had only collected unhappy masks, and there were all kinds of them—death masks, faces of angry gods and mischievous devils. The sight of their ill-will always gave me the shivers. I suspected Max liked them not only because they matched his general mood these last few years, when he started collecting them, but also because they represented something to hide his true face.

Now I realized I'd probably never known my husband at all, throughout the twenty-two years of our marriage. Certainly not as well as Gillian knew her half-brother.

And now he was back in town.

Was that what Detective Hennesey wanted to tell me?

Pushing those thoughts aside, I tried the door. Much to my surprise, it was unlocked. I breezed into the office. All right, I was here, but the police were not. There was no crime scene tape.

At first, the office looked the same, as if Max had only left a few days ago, on a research trip, perhaps. I shuddered and leaned across the desk to plug the waterfall's cord into a nearby outlet. Someone had kept the ceramic bowl full of water, and now it bubbled to life, as easy as that. I wished someone could plug in my cord and bring me to life. Water spurted and splashed over a flow of pebbles and filled the tiny room with a greater sense of peace and tranquility than I'd experienced for some time.

Focus, Nell, Master Hwang's voice reminded me in my head, *on your inner reservoir of strength, and you will be at harmony with the world.*

I never knew exactly what he meant by that, but I did know that the only way I was going to be at harmony with anything was to get my life back to something resembling normal. I couldn't put off facing Max's office any longer.

I was wrong. The office wasn't the same as it had been before. A box, displaying the logo of an imported Mexican beer, sat beside the desk, containing an unwieldy amount of mail, waiting for someone to do something with it. Not me. Leaving the nine months' worth of mail in a box left the surface of the desk relatively clear. The desktop held a blotter-sized calendar, showing last year's month of November, when time stopped for Max in this office. Beside the calendar sat the World's-Best-Dad mug Terra had given him one Father's Day. Instead of using it for coffee, he'd used it to hold pens and pencils.

One of them was a shiny, gold pen, which stood out from all the cheap ballpoints. I lifted it from the mug, and when I saw "Callahan Enterprises" engraved on its side, the pen slipped from my fingers and thudded onto the blotter. Callahan Enterprises wrote my paycheck. I stared at my boss's pen lying there on November as if it were a thing of evil.

Max, apparently, had a connection to my boss, Arlo Callahan. Had my husband left town to avoid the same fate my predecessor had suffered? I wondered if Callahan had known all along that I was Max Gannon's wife, and if that was why he'd been eager to hire *me*.

Questions danced around in my mind like one of my opponents on the balls of his feet, waiting to strike. Blinking, head bent, I felt dazed as if I'd been hit with a ridge hand to the head. Who was this man, my boss, really?

Heart rate accelerating, I bent down to snatch up a handful of Max's most recent mail. Among the assorted pieces, a business-sized envelope had a return address of a post office box in Frisco. I wasn't aware of any dealings Max had had with anyone in that mountain community.

I ripped it open and pulled out an invoice dated from last February. Written in a neat handwriting was the amount of five thousand dollars for "services rendered" for a period of ten days last September and October, shortly before Max's disappearance. How odd that he was being billed *now*.

While I was mulling this over, the office door creaked. In the briefest of seconds between that first sound and the door's opening, I whirled around and threw my mystery bookstore bag on top of the mail I'd pulled out of the beer box.

"Ma'am?" said Hennesey. "Good of you to come down."

"Well, Detective, I'm always eager to help," I said looking up at him. He was dressed in jeans and a T-shirt—no uniform nor tidy plainclothes slacks and polo shirt this time. His casualness fit his straw-like mop of hair better.

"I know you are, ma'am, and I appreciate that, regardless of... Oh, never mind."

"What's happened? And why are you here instead of campus police?"

"They're cooperating with our investigation by giving us access. That's where you come in."

"Me? What investigation? You mean about Alice's fire? But Detective, I don't believe Alice had any connection to the university. This is Max's old office, after all."

"Exactly. But Professor James has been using it ever since your husband left town last November."

My knees went weak beneath me. "Jackson is dead, isn't he? That's what you're investigating."

"His identity hasn't been released yet, but yes, I am afraid so. How did you know?"

I bit my tongue before revealing that I'd blabbed to the journalist. "He came to visit me, and then there was that accident."

One of his eyebrows lifted. "How well did you know him?"

"Not at all. Only through Max. At faculty parties. And then again day before yesterday, shortly after his release from the hospital..." I confessed everything except about the journalist. I told the detective about Jackson's appearance at the studio, how he'd been looking for Felix's fireproof box of money and was worried that someone was chasing him, thinking he had the money.

Hennesey listened silently, thoughtfully. He offered no comment, nor took any notes, as his partner always did. When I was done, he glanced around Max's office and said, "Can you identify your husband's belongings? It will help us to catalogue the rest, as belonging to Professor James."

"That's it?"

"Look around. Can you tell if anything has been disturbed?"

Masks on wall, check. Waterfall, check. Mug of pens, check. Beer box of mail, check. I pointed it all out to him.

"Anything that doesn't belong?"

"How would I know about the rest?"

Hennesey sighed. "What about the painting over there?"

He nodded at a small western landscape on the wall above the stuffed chair in one corner, where I knew Max used to take naps. I had been so filled with the angst of loss from the reminders of other memories that I hadn't even noticed the painting.

"I have no idea where that came from," I said. "I've never seen it before."

"Was there something different there before?"

"I don't know. I'm pretty sure the wall wasn't blank. Gillian would know better. She's the one who decorated here. You'll have to talk to her, although she's in a meeting now." I walked over to the sofa to study the painting closer. Its signature read Felix Todd. "This must belong to Jackson. He admired Felix's work. I'm sure I've never seen it before."

Hennesey made no comment, but went on. "Are there any knives in your husband's collections? You could save us time."

My heart thudded as my mind whirled through the connections. I could guess where he was going with this, and I blurted out my outrage. "You think Max killed Jackson? You're wrong. The chef, Dominic LePuc thought Max had stolen one of his knives, but he's wrong, too." Even to my ears, I sounded whiny. Maybe I was the one who was wrong. "You should check out LePuc's."

"Already been there. Robinette LePuc was one of the work-study students who used this office, and we wanted to ask her about the large packets of cash we found in your husband's filing cabinets."

I sucked in my breath. There was Robinette's name again. "So, Jackson *did* have the money all along. He must've hidden it here, thinking no one would search for it here."

"Except for your husband. We believe that your husband and Professor James were partners."

"Partners in *what*? They were friends, but what are you

implying? The cash you found here came from something illegal? Like drug smuggling? Just because of Max's long-term habit of crossing the border?"

A vein throbbed in Hennesey's temple, but his face remained deadpan. He wasn't going to tell me, so I went on with my speculation. "Or maybe you think the cash came from black market sales of marijuana?"

Needles of ice prickled through me as a new thought occurred to me. Alice was involved in it. That's why she'd run away. I kept that thought to myself. She was my best friend. I couldn't betray her.

But if she was involved in black market sales, then I hadn't known her at all, either.

Hennesey folded his arms and stood silent, either thinking about black market issues or waiting for me to go on.

I might not have to betray my friend at all, not if her employee Robinette had given her away. "What did Robinette tell you?" I blurted out, when the cop's silence got to me.

Hennesey frowned. "We didn't have a chance to speak to her. She was rushed to the hospital before we got there, from an overdose of edibles."

Sixteen

"I'M SORRY," SAID the woman at the hospital's reception desk. She wore a name tag that identified her as Betty, a volunteer. "The doctor has ordered no visitors other than family. Are you family?"

I shook my head, feeling heavy with dread. I was sort of family to Robinette's brother; maybe that would count. I decided not to press my luck. "Could I have a word with her doctor, then? Or at least with her brother?"

"Have a seat in the waiting area," Betty said with a kindly smile, "and I'll see what I can do."

I thanked her and found a seat strategically placed where I could watch the comings and goings from the rotating circle of the main entrance all the way down the tiled hall to the main elevators.

Ten minutes later, Dad stormed through the revolving doors, impatiently pushing against the glass cage, in a futile attempt to make it release him faster. He saw me almost as soon as I saw him. With keys jingling from his waist, he trotted over to my side. "Nellie! *Here* you are. Finally!"

"Hi, Dad. Have a seat and take a deep breath. What's up?"

"Jesus H. Christ."

Uh-oh. I was in trouble. Then I remembered that Terra had

warned me hours ago—last night?—something about "Gramps" phoning. He'd sounded "mad."

"Sorry, Dad. I guess I forgot to call you back, didn't I?"

"You guess? You *guess*? Dang it all, Nellie, you want me to have a stroke? It's not easy with your mother gone and your brothers off to Timbuktu."

"D.C., Dad. And Portland."

"Same difference."

My brothers were trying to make a living, same as me. "I know. I miss them, too."

If we were lucky, we saw them every other year. That left me—and Terra, too—as Dad's only family. Luckily, he didn't have to have a companion as Mrs. Harris had had.

Dad grunted and flung himself down onto the chair next to mine. "I heard it on the scanner, you know. About that car wrecking in the alley behind your place. And I knew right away that wasn't right. Something was up. You didn't call back, but at least I talked to Terra and knew you were still alive. Then when you didn't call and didn't call, I finally called Terra, and she called Gillian and heck-fire-knows who else until she tracked you down here. You were on your way to the hospital, and I thought 'oh lord, no'. So I came right away. You checking yourself in?"

"No, Dad. It's not like that at all. I'm fine. I've just been busy, helping Alice. Sorry for any misunderstanding." I kept my own voice calm in an attempt to calm him.

"You want to tell me how in the heck that man getting killed in a car wreck has anything to do with helping Alice?"

"It doesn't. That man was hurt in Alice's fire, that's all. It's so sad. He survived the fire but not the highways."

"It was an alley, not a highway."

"It was driving, all the same." I decided to let Dad think it was an accident and not a knife wound that had actually killed Jackson.

I patted his hand and told him why I was here—to support one of my students in his crisis. But it didn't stop there. I filled Dad in on my little chats with Jackson and Erica and Dominic and the lady at the gallery downtown. And didn't my old-lady neighbor Pearle, the one with the garden, sound like a lovely person? I wanted Dad to feel included in my activities—although not all of them. Max's antics would anger him, the guy in the Jeep would worry him, and the journalist would annoy him, so I left out any mention of them.

I was wrapping up my edited version of the story when the elevator pinged open and Elliott walked out. "Ms. Letterly? Some nurse said that you were down here and wanted to see me."

"Elliott! I'm so sorry to hear about your sister. How is she?"

"Bad." His face looked pasty white. "She's really sick. She hasn't barfed in a while, though, so they think she's going to be all right. Mom's up there with her now."

"And your dad?"

"My dad isn't the same as her dad, but neither one of them is here. I guess they're too busy to care."

Dad snorted. "Told you, didn't I?"

I patted Dad's arm to hush him and then spoke to Elliott soothingly. "I'm sure they have their reasons, and they'll be here shortly. The police told me it was edibles. Why did she take so much? Wasn't there a warning about not taking any more than a small amount?"

"See?" Dad said. "Nothing but trouble, that's what."

Elliott tipped his head sideways at Dad. "She didn't know it was going to poison her. Alice's boyfriend gave it to her. You know, that dude who hangs around in the alley and gives weed to the cat? His name is Jack, and he calls it 'cannabis for kitties'."

There's a whole new industry...

* * * * *

Alice—not Robinette, as Gillian had guessed—was Jackson James's girlfriend. I kept trying to wrap my head around that. And wondering why it was such a big secret. I felt a little miffed that Alice hadn't confided in me. Something more was going on than I could imagine. Maybe it had something to do with the reason Jackson had been acting so embarrassed. Pet cannabis? Maybe *that* was what all the lies were about.

Even after Elliott went back upstairs to his sister, I kept thinking about Jackson. And his cannabis. Why would he have fed marijuana to the cat? I would never know, now.

But it made me wonder... If cannabis was the real reason why Jackson was leaving the university. And if legalized marijuana had summoned Jackson's partner in crime—Max—back to Boulder with his blondes.

Grrr... I was becoming as suspicious and grumpy as my dad. Our presence here in the hospital wasn't helping matters.

I persuaded Dad to go home before the storm hit. I walked him out to his truck and kept going to my Ghia. My mind spun with questions.

Had the journalist, Steele Dickensen, been right? Was I a magnet for trouble, bringing together such previously unconnected people as Alice and Jackson? Either I was Typhoid Mary, or the black market that was springing up as a result of legalized marijuana had drawn unrelated people together and was killing them.

What also troubled me was that Alice, my best friend, hadn't been honest with me, despite my offer to help her. I didn't understand how she could've been so embarrassed that she wouldn't confess about her relationship with Jackson. Or about blowing glass to shape into pipes for smoking marijuana. I still couldn't believe she'd sell the stuff without the proper license and resort to black market dealing. Maybe she hadn't told me because she knew how I'd react. Sometimes I could come across as pretty righteous. It's all part of my job.

But if she wanted to sell the stuff, why not go through the proper channels and get the license? And why had she run away?

Did the deaths—no, the murders—have anything to do with all this?

Things had progressed so far that I no longer knew who my best friend was. I couldn't make sense of anything. At times like these, my sensei, Master Hwang pointed me to the path of clarity.

Twenty minutes later, the Ghia pulled into the parking lot of the strip center east of town, home to Master Hwang's studio. It was almost noon, a time that he reserved not only for his own workout with weights but also for private consultations with his long-term students, like me.

I pushed through the swinging doors, into the air-conditioned coolness of the studio where I'd left much of my sweat while training for black belt. I could still smell it, hanging here forever in the air.

As I stepped out of my sandals, I listened for the sound of the occasional clang of weights coming from the back room. Nothing. But I knew Master Hwang was here. He was always here. Besides, I felt a sense of peace and order wash through me. Here was the calm that had been lacking from the chaos of my last few days.

Leaving my sandals by the front door, I padded barefoot along the green indoor/outdoor carpeting. This time of day, the workout floor at the front of the studio was a vast, empty rectangular space. A door at the back of the studio led to a suite of private offices. Another door led to an exercise room with state-of-the-art equipment.

That's where I found Master Hwang. Short and wiry, my sensei had bypassed his fancy equipment and stood on his head with his bare feet propped like hammers against one wall. Upside down, his black eyes blinked, acknowledging my presence.

Waiting for him to finish his routine, I sat down on the floor in one corner of the room and folded my legs lotus-style. I opened my soul to absorb the calm energy that filled this place.

Finally, he kicked off from the wall and rolled into a ball that somehow back-flipped him upright onto his feet. He wrinkled his nose as he glanced at my own, which was still bruised and swollen. "For this you seek my advice?"

"Not exactly," I said. "Master Hwang, what do you do when you no longer know the people around you? People that you thought you once knew, and then you find out that all along you didn't really know them at all? Because they're not who you thought they were."

Or something like that. Boy, I did that badly. I always felt like a tongue-tied school child around my sensei.

174

His head tipped sideways as he peered at me and said, "You must learn to block better."

"The nose was an accident, Master Hwang. It doesn't matter."

"Yes, it matters. Use every tool, and you will progress along the path of self-awareness." As he spoke, he glided swiftly to a stack of hand pads, grabbed one in each hand, and held them up before me. "Alternating front punch, go."

He had trained me well enough that I knew not to question his instructions but simply to act. I lunged with my fist to punch the pad, but before it could connect, the pad wasn't there. Neither was he. I stumbled, momentum throwing me off balance, but I managed to stay upright, catching myself before an embarrassing tumble to my butt.

He clucked his tongue. "Footwork, Ms. Letterly. Remember your footwork."

Correcting my stance, I danced on the balls of my feet until he nodded his approval.

He shifted the position of one pad. "Slide-in front leg front kick, go."

Again I lunged, replacing my front leg with my back leg for support on the floor while my front leg snapped out a kick at the pad. But the pad wasn't there. Neither was Master Hwang.

He shook his head and beckoned me to follow him to the heavy bag, hanging on a chain from the ceiling. Lying on the floor nearby were a pair of gloves, which he motioned for me to slip on. All the while that I Velcroed, he kept reminding me about footwork.

"Two minutes," he said, glancing at the clock on the wall. "Go."

Oh drat. Two minutes didn't sound like much, but at full capacity of non-stop assault, it felt like forever on the bag. My dancing feet had to constantly move, and all the while, I kept alternating between a variety of punches and kicks, each one precise. Each one executed with enough force to level an adult opponent.

By thirty seconds I was panting, and I still had a long way to go.

I had a long way to go helping Alice, too. First, I had to find her.

By one minute, my heart raced and every muscle in my body burned.

I also had to find out why Alice had run. *On the run*, Erica had accused. *In hiding*, Terra had suggested. *Afraid for her life*, I imagined.

At ninety seconds, I would've quit, if not for Master Hwang watching me. I felt twice as heavy on my feet, and my lungs had surely emptied of all oxygen.

I suspected marijuana. The fire would have destroyed such evidence, and after all, we'd all smelled smoking pot at demo practice the night of the fire.

"Time," Master Hwang mercifully said.

I fell away from the bag, sucking in air and shaking life back into my limp appendages.

"With better footwork, you find your path," Master Hwang said. "Only when you become self-aware can you see others as they truly are."

I nodded and peeled off the gloves. I felt more aware of my pulsing, pounding heart than ever before. Bowing deferentially, I backed out of the exercise room. I felt aware of my lungs, too.

They were going to explode.

Once outside, on the sidewalk in front of Master Hwang's studio, I paused to drink in long and slow gulps of air. I stood taller. My head felt light, in a good way. The endorphins of post-exercise tingled through me, saturating me with a natural high.

I'd sucked in some clarity of mind, and now I thought I understood what Master Hwang had been trying to tell me in his veiled way. Constant movement, staying light on my feet would enable me to shift position at a moment's notice. Ninja-vanishing was a handy skill to develop, since someone—Max's old college roommate—was following me for reasons unknown.

Even now. The Jeep was parked two rows behind my Ghia.

Seventeen

I'D HAD ENOUGH. I marched over to the Jeep, expecting to see it gun the engine, screech its tires, and flee the parking lot before I could accost its driver. It didn't.

The Jeep sat empty.

I glanced around the parking lot, but no one that I could see was watching me. No dog, either. I scanned the cars, the sidewalks, the storefronts.

No one.

The Exterminator could be anywhere. I stormed back to my car and circled it, inspecting its paint job for more graffiti. There was none, though I decided I rather liked the original message, advertising me as the b-lady. Maybe I would keep it. Dropping to my knees, I peered underneath. No one hid there.

Good.

I fumed all the way home. I checked, and re-checked, my rearview mirror for the Jeep. It never appeared. That didn't necessarily mean the Exterminator wasn't somewhere back there, hidden in traffic, following me. My knuckles ached from gripping the steering wheel, and by the time I pulled into my parking space off the alley behind the studio, I thought my fingers had locked into place.

Even before I climbed out of the car, I saw the paper. Rolled

179

up, it inserted into the door handle of the back door to the studio. It was a flier, probably advertising someone's services, since there was no political campaign going on at the moment. Rubbing my knuckles, I thought it more likely they were sore from Master Hwang's heavy bag than my grip on the steering wheel.

When I snatched the paper out of the door handle and unfolded it, I saw right away that I was wrong. Oh, it was about services all right, but I was to be the servant. Its short, printed message to *me* read succinctly:

> Bring the T-bird to Mel's Mechanics in Nederland by 3 p.m. today. I've found a buyer for it. For your trouble, Mel will give you half the price, plus all the documents. I've signed over the house to you. No contest.
> Max

The paper rattled as a spasm swept through my body, shaking my fingers, buckling my knees, already weakened from my two intensive minutes on Master Hwang's bag.

I had to use both hands to stop the words from dancing around on paper. Maybe there was more to the message if only I looked harder. If I gripped the note even tighter, until it ripped, maybe the rest of the message would magically appear.

But that was all there was to it.

He gave no explanation of where he'd been these last nine months. No apology for putting Terra, Gillian, and me through hell. No "dear" or "love." Not even a "please" before the command "bring." No suggestion for how I'd get home after delivering his car to Nederland. The content of the letter was printed in his favorite, crisp, no-nonsense font, typed impeccably without error. It was so Max-like, right down to the heavy signature from his favorite signing instrument, a medium-point black pen. And it was Max's signature, that was for sure.

This could be no hoax. I recognized his style.

My fingers cramped from gripping the piece of paper. It was true, then. Max was here. In town. Perhaps he'd even been the one behind all the mysterious events plaguing me these last few days. Evidently, he was trying to keep information hidden from someone. Certainly from me.

* * * * *

The house would be all mine!

I wrapped my fingers tighter around the steering wheel of Max's T-bird and wished I could be almost anyplace else than here, in the driver's seat. Better, even, to be in the midst of my black belt test. But it was only a short jaunt into the mountains, and it would be well worth it to finally get Max out of my life, once and for all. Not to mention the much needed money. And the house! I could sell it. Pay off the mortgage. Get out of debt.

Terra would want to move back into it.

I scanned the sky. The clouds that had lowered around the mountains all day now looked angry and black with greenish underbellies, hinting at hail. I did not relish the thought of lightning bolts bouncing off these granite rocks surrounding me.

It was less than twenty miles up the canyon from Boulder to Nederland, but in bad weather it could be dicey.

And the Thunderbird wasn't exactly a car built for rain-slickened roads.

This model came out towards the end of the T-bird's production run. A beautiful car. And it was great, sitting in a car collection. Terrible in bad weather, though. Even worse if the bad weather was in a mountain canyon with sharp bends, cliffs, and steep inclines.

But the house would be all mine!

My bag sat on the seat beside me, the note resting on top, luring me on. Pulling off the side of the road before I hit the narrows of the canyon, I reached for my cell phone in my bag. Reception flat-lined. I opened the door and climbed out of the car to seek more bars somewhere along the embankment. The wind nearly whipped the car door from my grip, but I clung on. Don't damage the goods now, I thought.

Finally, reception wavered from no bars to one. I punched in Gillian's contact, tucked the phone between my ear and my shoulder, and listened to it ring. And ring. Then, Gillian's recorded voice whispered with sultry instructions to have a good day. As if in defiance of her wish, a gust of wind slammed into me. I was definitely not having a good day.

"Jill!" I gasped. "It's me. Nell. Pick up, won't you?"

I waited, staring through the window of the car. The note sat there on the seat, but I didn't need to retrieve it to see the words. I remembered them.

It amazed me the things I would do for the promise of money now that I had to pay all the bills...

"Nell?" Gillian finally said to me. "I just got in, and I thought I recognized your voice on the phone. You'll never guess what happened to me—"

"Jill, listen to me." I lowered my voice to a harsh register. I had to, in order to counter the rising tone of her song and to get her to pay attention to me.

"Speak up, I can't hear you."

It wasn't the connection. It was me. I was whispering as if someone might overhear. Would my amateur sleuthing never stop? It would all be over, I figured, as soon as I finished with Max. "I'm in the canyon," I shouted.

"Which canyon? What on earth are you doing there?"

"I'm on my way to Nederland."

"Oh." She sounded disappointed. "You could've waited for me, and I would've gone with you. But on second thought, I couldn't have gone this afternoon, anyway. Or tomorrow, either."

Darn. So much for obtaining a promise of rescue from Gillian. I would have to take the bus back. I had no idea how often it ran.

"Oh, Nell, you'll never guess!" Her voice was singing again.

I sighed, knowing she wouldn't listen to me, not in her present frame of mind, no matter what I had to say, not until she'd said her piece. "Okay, tell me. I give up. What's happened that's got you so excited?"

"Silly, I'm not excited. I really don't care, but I thought it might help you, so I agreed."

"You agreed to *what*?"

Either she yawned, or the wind was now speaking to me over the phone line. "I have a date with Jimmie Condo."

"But he's old enough to be your father!" I was shouting, and it wasn't to compensate for the wind's howl.

"Nell, you can be positively old-fashioned sometimes."

"Someone has to be," I muttered.

183

"What? I'm having trouble hearing you. Look, if I can get to know him better, I might find out something useful for you. Although I can't really believe he'd actually try to burn your friend Alice's house just to acquire her business, can you?"

"No."

When I failed to elaborate, because I was wondering how to tell her, or even if I should tell her the news about Max, she continued. "I only agreed to this date for your sake, you know."

"I'm sure you did."

"I can change it. I don't have to go. It's not that important."

I could visualize her square jaw, clamped with determination to show her indifference. She believed that what she said was true, despite the way her heart had sung through the tone of her voice. I shook my head and grumbled, "Don't change it on my account."

"Hello? Nell? Do you hear that static on your end? Why don't you try calling back?"

"No!" Somehow I felt that if I lost this connection to her, I'd lose my lifeline to safety. Probably irrational, but with an intensifying storm howling around me, it seemed a reasonable enough fear.

"I can't hear you!"

But I could hear her loud and clear. I stared at the note on the seat. I couldn't be the one to let Gillian know the truth about her assholian half-brother. He hadn't cared enough about any of us to let us know that he was alive. He'd deliberately put all of us through hell these last nine months.

"Nell? Are you still there?"

"Yes, Jill," I said softly.

"What'd you want, anyway?"

"Nothing. I just wanted to let you know I'm on my way to Nederland. You'll be there for Terra, right?"

The connection dropped before she could respond, but I knew she'd watch out for Terra. She always did. Punching the phone off, I stumbled down the embankment to the Thunderbird, where I wrestled the wind for the car door.

The wind won in that instant, whipped open the door and snatched the note out of the car. The paper shot outside into the storm and sailed away, dodging the first raindrops that splattered like heavy bullets.

* * * * *

When I crested the last hill, a curtain of rain slanted sideways, streaming faster than the windshield wipers could keep up. The clouds had descended so low that I couldn't even see the reservoir below me. I knew it was there.

Slowing the car, I considered pulling off until the rain let up. The Thunderbird wasn't built for slick roads, not like my Ghia. But it was only water, with a little hail thrown in. Not snow. And I could see well enough. Besides, I wanted to get this task over and done with, send Max on his way, collect my check and signed papers before Mel closed shop for the day. Then I would catch my bus back to Boulder. So I crept forward, rolling down the long slope toward the mountain town. It was a gradual slope, but downhill all the same. I tapped the brakes to go even slower.

The car jerked as the rear tire broke loose to the right, pointing the nose of the car to the left. I was aimed into oncoming traffic and the reservoir far below.

Coaxing the wheel to the right, I pulled out of the skid before things got worse, and then started to breathe again.

I leaned closer to the wheel, as if my extra alertness would keep the car moving in a straight line. But mountain roads are never straight. And this road bent ahead, just at the edge of my visibility. As I eased the wheel gently into its turn, a boulder about the size of a large soccer ball tumbled down the muddy embankment and into the path of the Thunderbird. I had to swerve. Hard.

The car careened too fast around the bend, bumped and rattled over loose rocks. I was vaguely aware of headlights through the fog as I fought the car's skid. Motion whipped me against my seatbelt, and finally the car landed sideways in a ditch, lurching to a sickening, crashing stop against a muddy bank.

Oh god.

At least it was better than landing in the reservoir. My heart raced, and I took several gulps of air to still my trembling. My fingers felt frozen in place to the steering wheel.

A tapping sound on my window jolted me out of my stupor. A man's face peered through the window at me. With his non-tapping hand, he held on tight to a fedora atop his head. "You all right, miss?" He was shouting.

I blinked and realized my mouth was gaping. I shut my mouth and nodded. Dazed, I stared at the cracked windshield in front of me. Through its splintered web I made out a parked vehicle in front of me.

It was a Jeep.

"You sure you're okay?" Jeep-Man asked. His voice drawled,

making complex syllables out of simple ones. "You don't look so good."

I sat there, catatonic, my fingers frozen to the shaft of the window crank. I couldn't see them, but I knew the plates on his car would read XTRMN8.

"You got a cell phone, miss?" He cast a worried glance at the traffic creeping past us.

The doors were locked, I told myself. The window was only lowered enough to talk through. I felt the slow, steady beat of my heart as I came back to life. "Y-yes. I'll call a tow truck."

"I'll wait with you," he said with a dimpled smile.

I blinked. How could someone who thought of himself as an exterminator have dimples? I shook my head vigorously. "I'll be okay. I *am* okay. Really."

"Wouldn't want you to go into shock." He walked around the car and reached for the door handle on the passenger's side. "Look, you can trust me," he shouted above the storm, pulling his windbreaker apart to reveal a clerical collar.

Father or not, he was still a stranger. And I wasn't going to let a stranger inside my car. I popped the lock on my door and climbed out, where I judged it safer to play in the fringes of skidding traffic.

Eighteen

I MISSED the bus.

Some time later, I straggled into Suki's, a new southwestern restaurant a block off the main drag of the mountain town. The place teemed with the chatter of its patrons. A highway patrol officer had given me a lift into town.

None of this would've happened if not for Max. I toasted him silently with a sip of my raspberry tea. Then I took another sip to celebrate my extreme good fortune. Not only had I lived through the accident but I'd also had the Thunderbird towed directly to Mel's. Job done. Yay.

But it had been after three, and Mel had gone home already. So I got no check. No signed papers.

Oh, sure, I could've waited for a later bus. But I remembered Jackson's invitation and supposed the offer still stood, posthumously. Quite frankly, I felt too beat up from all of today's car excitement to see the inside of that canyon again anytime soon. A peaceful dinner, followed by a short hike up to Jackson's home, and a little mountain solitude was too irresistible. In the morning, I would find Mel, get my check and signed papers, and be on my way again.

The thin front door burst open, spinning piñatas into a dancing frenzy on their strings. Raindrops whisked inside and sparkled in the glow from the fireplace. Warm odors of tortillas and mesquite hung in the air. A lanky figure in black slinked inside, and the next thing I knew, Kingsley Park, the Exterminator, slid into my booth.

Kingsley's collar had bought him permission to stick to my side like an unwanted burr after the highway patrol eventually showed up at the accident scene. By the time the officers were done with me, Father Park practically knew my life history. Maybe he knew the censored parts as well, since he was on the inside track with God.

I thought I'd shaken him. Too stunned for words, I looked up at him now and focused on the fedora. It didn't go with his black habit and white collar, but I was no expert on church things.

He must've noticed me staring at it because he reached up and lifted the damp canvas hat from his head, spraying raindrops across the table in the process. The shock of sun-bleached hair on top with gray sideburns wasn't any more comforting. "Nasty weather we're having out there. May I join you, Nell?"

"Hello, Father." I figured that with the restaurant more than half full, there was safety in numbers.

"You can drop the 'Father'." He tugged on his collar, adjusting it away from the red splotches appearing on his neck.

I studied him curiously and wished he weren't so ruggedly attractive. The creases on his suntanned face reflected a lifetime of adventures, and they'd left him with a careless and savvy bearing in the way he moved with such utter confidence. I couldn't imagine how a priest could experience more in life than the mother of a teenager. For all I knew, his activities ranged from diving with sharks to bicycling across the Alps.

He flagged down the waitress, who was covering too many tables for a sane person, and ordered a beer with the ease of someone accustomed to places like this. Then he leaned back against the cracked vinyl of his bench seat. He was far too relaxed to fit my image of a priest, but then, I'd never known any.

Obviously, he wasn't a priest. Did he wear the get-up to make me think I could trust him?

"So," I said, lifting my cup to hide the suspicion that must be showing on my face. "Where are you from, Father?"

"Boulder," he said.

"Boulder! Imagine that! So am I!"

He nodded and chuckled. "Yes, I know. You told the officer, remember?"

I scowled. I wasn't going to let him twist this conversation around to be about me. "What church do you practice in, Father? Or maybe that's the wrong way to put it?"

He watched a group at a neighboring table rock back in their chairs and laugh. "It's a small church. You probably haven't heard of it."

"Try me."

"Okay, it's called 'Our Mother of the Shepherds'."

He was right. I hadn't heard of it. "Where is it?"

He pulled his attention back to me and studied me for an agonizing moment. His eyes were the shade of a Douglas fir with little dappled specks of sunlight. "It's one of the many new ones being built out east. Land is more easily available out there, you know."

I nodded. Something was making me feel warm inside. The tea, or the mesquite surroundings, or the false sense of security

191

from the throng so near at hand. Or maybe it was the greenish amber flecks in his eyes.

"Although," he added, "the north side of town is going through a lot of development, too. Where you live."

"Actually, I'm in transition," I said, then bit my tongue. Babbling, spilling too much information, was a nasty effect he was having on me.

"Because of your day job?" he asked with those eyes again. "Or is it your soul?"

Looking around for the waitress to distract this man, I had a feeling that Kingsley Park already knew the answer. "They're one and the same," I said, bringing my own gaze back to him. "I teach karate." I let that sink in, thinking it was a good line to squelch potential advances into my soul. In a minute, this man would suddenly remember he hadn't fed the dog, and he would throw a ten on the table and flee before the waitress could return with his beer.

"Is that so?" he said instead, leaning on his elbows and bringing those eyes and dimples of his even closer to my face.

"Uh-huh." I quivered inside like a shimmering aspen leaf.

"Hmmm." He stroked his chin. The stubbles were noticeably longer than they'd been a couple hours ago up there on the mountain with the highway patrol. "Would that be a reason to pick up an enemy or two?"

My heart skipped a beat. "What do you mean?"

But he didn't answer me. He murmured words of gratitude when he spied the waitress bringing his beer.

The air in this toasty room, particularly over my booth, chilled. This man knew something, and he was trying to hide it. I should've gotten up and left right then, but the promise of fajitas kept me imprisoned there. Besides, I'd never been very good at making the wisest choices.

"What do you mean that I have an enemy?" I repeated, when the waitress was gone and Kingsley had taken a long swallow of beer.

He wiped froth from his upper lip with the back of his hand. I suppressed the urge to pass him a napkin. "Your near-miss with that rock slide this afternoon," he said. His eyes looked sad as they searched mine. There seemed to be more he wanted to say.

I decided to give him the opportunity. "Why have you been following me?"

His mug thudded down on the table and completely missed the paper coaster. "Following you? I...don't understand."

"Sure you do." I spread my elbows on the table and leaned on them. "You've been following me around Boulder. And now here you are. Convenient, isn't it? What do you want? It has to do with my ex-husband, doesn't it? Do you double as a reporter? Or have you taken on the salvation of my soul as some sort of special project? A test you have to pass before moving on to the next level of priesthood?"

His cheeks flushed, and he turned his neck so that his Adam's apple bobbed free of the stiff collar. "I'm sure you have me mistaken for someone else."

"No, I don't," I lied. "It's you, all right." *The Exterminator.*

He pushed an impatient hand through a lock of his golden hair and changed the subject. "After the tow truck dropped your car off at that repair shop, I, uh, found an opportunity, shall we say, to take a closer look at the area of the rock slide."

"I guess you're good at shadowy work."

His flush deepened. "I think you'll be interested in what I discovered. The ground had recently been disturbed, dislodging the rocks that slid down the hillside and struck your car."

"Yeah, it was a disturbance called 'rain'."

"There were footprints, too." Kingsley paused, studying my face, trying to penetrate the inscrutable mask I'd summoned into place. "And marks dug into the ground, probably made by a shovel. It looked like someone dug those rocks loose and shoved them down the hill at you. Don't you get it? Someone's trying to hurt you. I thought you needed to know. Now, who knew you'd be driving *that* car up there at that precise hour?"

God in heaven. My mouth dropped open in an attempt to find an answer, a name that wouldn't be Max's. The fajitas arrived then, sizzling on their metal plate, but I was no longer hungry.

* * * * *

He never admitted he'd been following me, but he didn't deny it, either.

After dinner, he offered to drive me back to Boulder. Was he kidding?

But here's the kicker: I almost took him up on it. If he was the one hurling boulders at me, then why would he warn me of it? At least that's the way I reasoned—maybe in truth, it was the green flecks in his eyes.

Luckily, my good sense prevailed. I paid my bill, said goodnight, and walked away from his stream of protests. I slipped out into the night. The rain had let up, but it was still damp and drippy. Mist tingled my face. I ducked around to the back of the rustic building before Kingsley, the Exterminator, could follow. Weaving past cabins and sheds, sprinting from one block to the next, I made my way to the outskirts of the mountain town. No Jeep headlights patrolled. I'd dodged him. Inhaling deeply, I slowed my pace down to a brisk stride. It was another mile or so before the side road to Jackson's place headed up into the forest.

I had a lot to mull over. The solitude of wooded mountains always worked like a salve and helped me figure out whatever needed figuring.

Part of me actually missed Kingsley's company, despite the rational side of my brain that reminded me that he was a stranger. I'd told Terra never to accept rides with strangers. I should act no differently.

Although, the way I figured, Kingsley was no longer a stranger. Strange for a priest impersonator, maybe, but after you've helped someone build fajitas, you've established the beginnings of a serious relationship.

Another part of me was already absorbing the restorative powers that eked out of this dark and wooded place. Positive energy flowed from the whispering Ponderosa pines standing guard over the road, and that energy beckoned me further into the forest that buffered Jackson's mountain home. Civilization was only a stone's throw away, but you would never know it up here.

Jackson's house, I remembered, sat alone in the forest, perched like the beached prow of a boat on a ridge overlooking a valley. His nearest neighbor was a mile away. I liked it that way, being alone. It gave me a chance to think without the distractions of other people's problems around me.

Maybe that was the real reason why Max had always disapproved of me. Because of my aloofness. Disapproval was one thing, but wanting to hurt someone—heck, maybe even *kill* someone—well, that was something else. Despite our differences, Max would never want to kill me. I knew that to be true, no matter how much he disapproved of me. Twenty-two years of wedded misery had taught me that much. He'd fled from all that. And even if I was wrong (which I usually was, according to Terra), he would never have attempted to kill me by prying rocks loose to crash into his prized Thunderbird.

But could I really be sure about that, when the evidence suggested otherwise? If one could believe a priest impersonator who moonlighted as an exterminator.

Then, there was the note. Max was the one who'd lured me up here. It had clearly been his signature. However, I reminded myself, it wouldn't have been difficult for someone else to trace his simple but bold, three-letter signature.

I stopped, sucking in a breath of moist air. Of course. Why hadn't I seen it? The note was a forgery. I had been wrong, feeling so certain that it was Max's signature.

Someone had forged his signature.

Whoever had written the note had killed before. He'd killed Jackson. And Felix. Maybe even Max. Now he—or she—was after me.

My heart rate sped up, easily accomplished between the altitude and my nerves on edge. Forest hemmed me in. From the distance came the occasional hoot of revelry, muted by the low cloud ceiling. Another fool like me must've been outside, only he was playing, while I was running.

Always running away.

Shivering uncontrollably, I knew I had to stop running. I couldn't continue to hide. I had to face my dragon.

The road to Jackson's house looped through a stretch of forest ahead, past some turn-offs I didn't remember. Hesitating, I glanced back over my shoulder in the direction of the hooter and the town in the distance. Was that a car I heard? The route of the looping road would take me through unpopulated sections of the forest. Well, I'd wanted to be alone, hadn't I?

I plowed along the road and told myself I wasn't completely alone, anyway. There were a few isolated houses tucked into the forest. Besides, if anyone attacked me here, I was ready.

Ahead, I saw the skeletal outlines of a new house being framed, and I hurried my pace. A flash of movement made me turn my head, but I saw nothing except mist licking against the erect timbers of the house-to-be. My peripheral vision was fooling me. Probably another failing condition of middle age.

Then I froze in my tracks, feeling the sting of surrounding stillness on my cheeks.

Whoever had forged Max's note, I realized, was the owner of the footprint Kingsley had seen, and he'd dug up the boulder to send tumbling down the bank beside the road to smash into the Thunderbird. He'd wanted to kill *me* while making it appear that my husband was alive, in hiding, and the guilty one. Who would've done that?

Someone close to Max. A colleague. Or an ex college roommate.

But Jackson was dead, and the roommate... I'd left him behind, thank goodness.

Peripheral movement once again caught my eye. I whirled toward it and stared directly at the wall of pine trees, daring one of them to move. A branch waved at me, and a wolf-like animal emerged from the underbrush. Tags jingled, and I relaxed a tiny bit. It was a dog. The dog moved briskly, between a trot and a run, as if he hadn't yet decided whether or not to attack. Standing my ground, I glanced around, looking for his owner, but no one else was in sight.

The dog approached me whether or not I wanted him to. Now I could see that he was a lot leaner than a wolf. He had the upright ears and stubbed-off snout of a boxer, and he looked very puzzled, with a fat tongue poking out the front end and a stubby tail motionless at the rear. He gave me a lingering sniff, probably interested in Sammy the ferret's smell on me, set his brow into a mass of wrinkles, then gave my hand a sympathetic lick.

I returned his favor with a pat on the head, told him to go home, then resumed my walk. He followed a step or two behind. His presence comforted me, but I had to stop again and tell him to go home. He continued following me.

"So," I said to the dog, "you like walking in the rain, too?"

He didn't answer, but the trees groaned under a surge of wind. We both hurried our pace. Someone had let this dog out to walk himself on a night like this. Or maybe the dog was lost. I wished I'd thought to keep a flashlight in my pocket, then I could read his tags and find out where he belonged.

Finally, I saw a light twinkling ahead through the edge of the forest. I breathed a sigh of relief and followed the last bend around to Jackson's house. Then I jerked to a stop, the wet night air burning my lungs. The driveway in front of Jackson's house remained empty, but a shadowy figure moved just beyond the reach of the light next to the garage door.

Nineteen

THE DOG STOPPED next to me, lifted his snout and sniffed the air. Then he suddenly charged ahead amidst a flurry of rattling tags.

Frozen in place, I suddenly felt sick to my stomach.

"There you are, Bruno," the man in black said from under cover of the shadows next to Jackson's wraparound deck. It was Kingsley's voice. He held out his arms, and the dog bounded to him, then did a dance before him.

Alarm flushed away my queasiness. I hadn't escaped him at all.

"Father, did you want something?" I asked, wishing he really was a priest. I lingered at the edge of the driveway and mentally reviewed some self-defense techniques. I would take him down if I had to.

"Forgive me for intruding." Kingsley brushed at the wet drops on his windbreaker, as if he expected to be invited inside. "My cabin's not far from here. I went back for the dog after dinner, and while I was out with him, I guess we got separated."

A likely story. I didn't think it was coincidence that he "found" me here, but how on earth had he managed to follow me without being seen? I thought I'd been so careful to give him the slip.

"You see," he went on, "I was preoccupied." He paused to scrape mud from his leather boots. "I...couldn't leave you without making a confession first."

"I thought you said you live in Boulder," I pointed out. The dog charged up the steps and clicked his toenails along the deck, exploring its length, pausing to sniff here and there.

Kingsley didn't respond to my reminder of his inconsistency. "I won't take much of your time," he said, instead.

Glancing over at the empty parking space, I realized he'd walked here with the dog. I couldn't very well suggest we go out for coffee for a chat. Had he planned it that way?

Clearly, he wanted me to invite him in.

Mind made up, I planted myself in the middle of the driveway and folded my arms across the rain-smeared front of my jacket. I could outrun him, if he got too close. "Okay, I'm listening. What did you want to say?"

He sat down on the first step and looked up at me with a hang-dog expression of sympathy. "Tell me," he said softly, "is there something you have that would benefit your husband if you were to die? Maybe an insurance policy?"

"Max didn't try to kill me, if that's what you're implying. He had his faults, but not that one. Why are you interested in him, anyway?"

Kingsley wagged his head. "I'm only trying to help you."

"Am I supposed to thank you? Tell me, Father, what's your angle? Do you strike up a deal with criminals? You save their victims' souls before they become victims? What do you get out of this? Brownie points with the big guy in the sky?"

He opened his mouth as if to say something in his defense, but he shut it again. No denial.

"Look, Father, you're wasting your time with me. I'm not a believer."

"I promise you, this is nothing to do with you, personally."

A single laugh exploded from me. "Do you expect me to believe that? You've told me that someone is trying to kill me, but no, it's nothing to do with *me*."

He sat there in the glow of the outdoor light, his cheeks ruddy with the damp chill of the air, and he took everything I hurled at him. I lowered my voice and went for the kill. "I think you know what else my husband was up to."

"It wasn't a coincidence," he said softly with a slight drawl. "I didn't just happen along up there on the mountain this afternoon. Yes, you were right—I *was* following you. Even around Boulder. And I learned enough about you that I knew you'd come up here tonight to Jackson's house."

With dread weighing me down, it took me a while to hear what he was telling me. I didn't know what to say, now that he'd confessed to my suspicions. Kingsley Park was the man in the Jeep. Had he exterminated them all—first Felix, and then Jackson? He was probably the person Alice was hiding from.

I shifted to the balls of my feet, ready to put some extra steps of distance between us. "So that's it? That's your confession?"

"Part of it." His cheeks deepened in hue, and he suddenly became interested in the pattern of puddles on the sidewalk. I was betting he wouldn't tell me the other parts.

"Mind telling me why you were following me? Am I on God's black list?"

He smiled and tried unsuccessfully to hide it. "I'm afraid I can't reveal that information. It would betray a confidence."

"Oh, sure." This news troubled me more than Max's betrayal.

"Never mind an invasion of *my* privacy."

Now his face took on a pained look, as if I'd just punched him in the solar plexus. "I'm sorry. I didn't mean—"

"How long has this been going on?"

"I can't tell you that, either."

Something was very wrong with this picture, I thought, taking a step backwards. I nearly jumped out of my skin when the dog woofed at his shadow. "Doesn't the church keep you busy enough? Since when do priestly duties involve following people?"

He didn't appear amused. "One more thing," he told the ground. "I shouldn't admit this." He looked up at me and sighed. "But I have to. I'm...not a priest."

His voice was so low I almost missed it.

"I knew that," I said, a little too quickly. "It's not seemly for a priest to drive a car with license plates that read 'exterminate'."

"It's not what you think." His body language stiffened as if with sudden conviction. "It's my slogan, that's all. I exterminate problems for my clients. I'm a private investigator."

"Sure." If he made any sudden moves towards me, I could easily sweep him and take him to the ground long enough to make my escape.

"Your husband hired me."

Well. Things were getting interesting. "I presume you're telling me this because you no longer work for Max?"

"Correct."

My defenses crumbled, and tears sprang to the corners of my eyes. "Why?"

"I'm telling you now because he hasn't paid me for the last—"

"No!" I screamed, or maybe cried, but either way, a drop of spittle arced through the air at him. "Why did Max hire you in the first place?"

Kingsley shrugged. "I guess he thought you were fooling around."

"You *guess*? Don't you know?"

"Maybe with one of your karate buddies."

Turning my back on him—he wasn't going to attack me—I nearly choked with disbelief. And what about Max? Was he not held accountable for the two blondes? Who knew how many others there were.

"Max doesn't approve of the things you do, does he?" Kingsley said softly behind my shoulder.

I sniffled. The dog barked again. "That's putting it mildly. If he thought I was having an affair, why didn't he just confront me? How dare he hire a private investigator!"

"I think he was hoping I'd find some embarrassing evidence that would force you to quit your martial arts training because he disapproved of it so much."

I shook my head. "But you couldn't come up with the evidence he wanted, so he wouldn't pay you?"

"I found evidence, all right."

"What? But I never—"

"It wasn't against you."

The meaning of his unsaid words took a full minute to register in my mind. It was *him*. Max. The cheater.

I whirled around to vent my anger at Kingsley, because he was available. "Why are you telling me these things? Are you expecting *me* to pay you for your disgusting information? Is that it? I didn't ask to hear it! I don't want to hear it!"

He shook his head sadly. "I'm sorry. When I found out that Max was carrying on with your neighbor, right under your nose—"

"Neighbor?" I gulped. "You mean *Celeste*?"

Kingsley tugged on his earlobe and nodded. "Anyway, the focus of my investigation changed after that."

"Are you sure?" My voluptuous neighbor drank too much at neighborhood barbecues and teased all the men. Of course it had been her. It had been *her* long, black hair I'd found on Max's lapels all those months ago. My feelings for Max had died long before that, and now I wanted to laugh aloud.

"I was intrigued," Kingsley continued, "because your husband seemed so obsessed. So different from the way he used to be when we went to college together."

So Jill was right when she thought the guy with the hairy legs looked familiar. She must've seen him hanging out with her big brother.

Kingsley sighed and pushed a lock of hair from his forehead. "After graduation I was on the fast track in Dad's management firm back east. Until a few years ago, when it hit me that I couldn't live that way any longer. So I left. Came out here to the mountains and hung my shingle. The P.I. business was a bit slow, but the skiing was great. When Max showed up last year, I thought he was doing me a favor. I'd intended to investigate corporate affairs—"

"In Nederland?"

"It was Frisco, actually, but can you think of a better place to live than anywhere in the mountains? Under other circumstances I'd have turned down Max's offer. Spying on spouses, that's messy. Not for me. But I had bills to pay, so I took the job."

"But why did you keep following *me*," I asked, "if Max hadn't paid you, and he'd dropped out of sight? Didn't you know he'd left the country?" I advanced on him, shaking my finger all the while. "What kind of investigator are you?"

"Not much of one," he said, holding his ground despite the blow I'd given him. He thought about it a minute, then cocked his head and gave me a wry smile. "So I guess it's not surprising that I'm breaking the confidence of a client, is it? Still, I expect to be paid, and when I sent Max an invoice last winter, he said he couldn't pay it right away, that it'd take time to move money around so *you* wouldn't know about the payment. I figured he was still working with that numbered account in the Caribbean, maybe the same one he'd had back when we were in college. That's where he hid money he'd siphoned off his wealthy family back east."

And had conveniently never told me about it.

"I agreed to wait," Kingsley continued, "because he's a buddy. Besides, I knew where to find him once he came back. Only he never returned. Meanwhile, my bills were stacking up, and I was in the process of moving my office closer to Boulder, where I thought I might find more business. I hoped someone might pay, you, maybe, if you'd closed out his affairs. Then I wondered if you were in on his scheme, if you knew where he was. That's when I started checking up on you. I'm really sorry now. It was routine stuff, that's all. And I did it because I hoped you might lead me to him. I didn't expect to find out instead that..."

He studied me, frowned, then the lines on his face softened. Dimples jumped out of the worried creases outlining his mouth.

"I don't know how to say this. I've known Max a long time. We were in the same fraternity. I know what kind of taste he's had in women, the way he's tried to control them. But you… You're different. I don't know. You're just not the kind of woman Max would've ever gone for."

When I failed to thank him, he continued. "I'm sorry. Guess I shouldn't have done it that way. I should've just asked you outright about Max, but I didn't. I made a mistake, and now I'm making another one by telling you these things." He paused to study the sidewalk again and dab his toes at the puddles.

"How do I know it wasn't *you* who rolled those rocks into the Thunderbird?" I said. "Considering that you were *there*."

He sighed. "You'll just have to trust me. I didn't do it."

We stared at each other silently for several more minutes.

"I'll get out of your life now," he said finally, "and I won't bother you again. I promise."

There was a certain finality to the deep breath he took. Then he strode along the sidewalk, toward the road. "Bruno," he called.

A tinkle of tags, and the dog clicked along the deck, down the steps, and padded over to Kingsley's side.

"Wait," I called.

He stopped and turned around.

"What time will you pick me up in the morning to drive to Boulder?"

Twenty

THE MAN AND his dog faded away into the dark of the forest. I stood there on the deck, watching, wondering what I had done. What on earth had possessed me to invite him back?

No worries. He was okay.

Hurrying to the garage, I punched in the code. H-i-g-h. The door lifted, and I ducked inside.

The garage smelled of cut grass, gardening tools, and gasoline. A pick-up truck fitted out with a small camper sat there in the dark. It didn't look like something Jackson would drive. Was someone else staying here? More likely, he let a friend park it here in exchange for a little help taking care of the property.

Another door led into the entry hall of the house. Hesitating there, clutching the knob on the open door, I couldn't shake the feeling that I was breaking into Jackson's home. He'd practically insisted I stay here, spelling out the code to me. I stared into the dark interior of the mountain home as the garage door rumbled shut behind me.

Someone's trying to hurt you, Kingsley had said. Maybe even worse.

Feeling stronger after hearing Kingsley's confession—he wasn't trying to kill me—I shed my wet jacket and shoes and groped my way through the dark interior.

Something musky in here.

It was the smell of an unfamiliar house, and it had been closed up too long. The smell of rain had slipped inside with me.

In the living room I flipped the wall switch, and brass and ceramic table lamps blazed with light at either end of the leather sectional.

Around another corner was a kitchen. Jackson's drop lights made a fashionable statement, leaving pools of light across the granite countertops. One such pool served as a spotlight on the black and chrome cappuccino-maker. A must for every gourmet cook's mountain retreat.

Next to it sat a woman's purse. Not just any purse. Alice's. I'd seen it before in Dad's guestroom.

Feeling relief drain from me, I stared at the ceiling. She must be upstairs now. *Of course* she would've come to this particular mountain home. I wanted to slap my head. I pictured Terra's eye roll and could almost hear her comment of "duh."

Elliott had said that Jackson was Alice's boyfriend. She'd wanted a place to hide, a place away from me. What had she said? She didn't want to "drag" me into her "mess." Her secret boyfriend's isolated mountain home was the perfect hiding place.

But she probably didn't know yet about Jackson's death. He'd died *after* Alice's chat with Hennesey.

Oh, poor Alice.

For about half a second I considered going up there right away, to break the news to her.

Then I realized that if she'd heard me enter through the garage, she could be on the phone now, calling the sheriff to report an intruder.

I rushed back to the entry hall and called up the stairs. "Alice? It's me, Nell."

There was no response.

"Alice? Are you okay?" I crept up the stairs.

A night-light plugged into a wall socket showed me three open doors. Inside the back bedroom, I saw a lumpy shape under the bedcovers and heard soft breathing. It was Alice. Poor woman. Sound asleep. She hadn't heard me after all. I decided to let her sleep. There was always time later to break the news about Jackson. And about Robinette, in the hospital.

I closed the door and tiptoed back downstairs.

Why hadn't my best friend talked to me, before dashing up here, for heaven's sake?

I needed a cup of tea after my own trek up here. I headed back to the kitchen, filled the kettle with water, and turned the burner on "hi."

The more I thought about it, the more I wondered. Who was Alice, really? What was she hiding?

Fuming more and more about her withdrawal, I stalked back into the living room, waiting for the water to boil for my tea. Paperback novels lay strewn across one end table. Alice had been here, all right. She had an account at the local used bookstore. I knew that much about her, at least.

I drifted over to the sliding glass doors. The night was silent, muted by the misty leftovers from rain. Chilly air seeped through the pane and drew me to it. I leaned my forehead against the glass, but it wasn't cold enough to cool my brow.

These glass doors with the surrounding deck had reminded me of the prow of a ship in Felix's "Mountain High" painting. The ship-like house in the painting overlooked a marijuana field. I wondered if Jackson had really grown marijuana here. I reached for a light switch behind the curtains, flipped it on, and stepped out onto the deck. The lights from the deck flooded the night but revealed nothing of the vegetation below.

I'd assumed Felix had taken artistic license, but maybe Jackson really *had* been growing marijuana on his property. It was isolated enough here in this mountain setting to avoid attention. But why? Why would he have done it and risk the scandal?

The kettle started to whistle, and I hurried back inside to answer its call. I slammed some kitchen cupboards around until I'd produced a pottery mug and Jackson's unlabeled canister of tealeaves. I gave them a sniff but couldn't determine from their herbal smell how much caffeine the tea might or might not contain. Not that it mattered. After the day's events, I would sleep, no problem.

Not finding a ball, I scooped the tealeaves directly into my mug, and then poured steaming water on top. I carried it back to the living room to let it steep, sat down on the sofa, and thumbed through the paperbacks.

Finally, I lifted my mug close to my nose and let its warm aromas drift into me as I sipped.

Yech.

What on earth kind of tea had Jackson stocked?

Given the cappuccino-maker, he probably hadn't been much of a tea man. But really. This was disgusting. I sipped again. I didn't recognize its flavor, but at least it was warm.

* * * * *

I did not intend to fall asleep, but I must've. Some time later, a groggy consciousness dripped slowly through me. Something seemed out of place. My brains felt like scrambled eggs. I'd dozed off over a book, apparently, and I hadn't even finished my tea. It had been one heck of a day, its memory slowly seeping back into my fuzzy awareness, but I shouldn't feel this groggy.

Something...in my tea.

I jerked upright, feeling instantly more alert. Yet, my limbs didn't want to work. Some sort of heaviness held me down, pinned me as if in a body hold.

Then I caught a whiff of...smoke.

I jerked some more and ended up rolling off the sofa along with the open paperback that had put me to sleep.

I had been reading, I was sure I had. But I didn't remember turning off the lights. Someone had turned them off for me.

Whyyyy?

No. The question was: *Whoooo?*

Pain was hammer-striking the inside of my head.

Where was that smoke coming from? It was ashes from the fireplace, dampened from the rain. I started to drift again.

Wait.

Had I turned off the stove? Oh crap.

I wrestled with the floor and struggled onto my knees. I did a Master Hwang and lifted an inconceivable amount of weights and pushed up onto my feet. Which way was the kitchen? I spun in circles and almost fell, undoing all my hard work.

There. A flickering light. Follow the light.

No! Not light. It was fire.

Fire.

Inside

211

The

House.

Adrenaline, thank god, must've started pumping, washing enough fuzz from my mind to function. I felt like a staggering, clumsy, brand-new white belt, but at least I was moving, searching for my bag, which held my cell phone.

Got to call 911.

Got to wake up Alice.

Why hadn't the smoke detectors gone off here in… Where was I, again?

I groped my way into the hall. Found my bag. Rummaged inside.

It was getting hard to breathe.

Was Alice still breathing? I had to find her. There were stairs here, somewhere.

Found the stairs.

Step after step…pushing, pulling…working as hard as in my black belt test…

"What is the nature of your emergency?" someone said in my ear.

"Alice! Wake up!"

"Ma'am, do you require assistance?"

I couldn't remember which bedroom Alice was in. I stumbled into the first one, but no one was there. "Alice?"

"Ma'am?"

The smoke thickened around me, or so I thought, and I managed to gasp to the woman in my ear, "Fire!"

"Ma'am, I need you to leave where you are at right now."

"Alice!" I lurched into the next bedroom, and the next one. "Ma'am…"

I staggered and stumbled until I found the shape in the bed. "Alice, wake up!" I tripped against the edge of the bed, grabbed onto my friend and gave her a shake.

"Mmmm," she said in her sleep and swatted at me with a limp arm.

Seeing my friend even groggier than me worked like a cold shower, slapping me awake. I dropped the phone into my bag, hooked to my shoulder, and raced to the bathroom, yanked towels off the bars and flung them into the sink, filling them with water. Returning, I wrung them out over Alice's head.

"Move!" I ordered, but she didn't.

I leaned down and lifted her to me, but she was too heavy for me to haul up onto my shoulders. So I dragged her instead, by the arms, plopping her onto the floor, sliding her dead weight across the carpet. The voice of the woman on the phone chattered all the while from my bag.

I managed to drag Alice on her butt all the way to the head of the stairs. "C'mon, honey, please wake up."

Together, buffered with towels, we rolled and tripped and slid down the stairs.

"What the hell?" she said when we landed with a thud of bruised tailbones to the bottom of the stairs.

Good. We were both still alive and more or less awake.

"We've got to get out of here," I said, throwing a towel over her face. "There's a fire. Fire trucks are on the way." Crouching toward the clearer air low to the floor, I backed into the front door.

It wouldn't open.

The doorknob burned my hand when I first touched it. Using my towel, I tried again, fighting to turn the knob. It wouldn't turn. Something jammed inside the lock. I sidekicked the door, summoning all the strength behind my hips, but the damned door wouldn't splinter.

"C'mon, there's another way out," I said, half-helping, half-hauling Alice into the living room to the sliding glass doors.

We covered our faces with towels, but light still dazzled my eyes, making me blink tears. The night sky through the windows lit up with fire. Fire jumped back and forth between the house and the rain-drenched vegetation outside.

The glass door slid open, and smoky air poured over us. Embers crackled, and the sound of moving fire roared in my ears.

"This way," said a man's voice. He stood on the deck surrounding the house, as if waiting for us. Even with a fuzzy mind on the edge of panic, I wondered where were the rest of the firefighters. There should be lots of hoses aimed this way.

"So glad to see you guys," I mumbled.

He grabbed my wrist and pulled me toward the wooden steps leading down to the hillside below the prow-end of the house.

That direction would lead us closer to the line of fire. I could see now that it was the hillside on fire, and not the house, at least not yet, or maybe not completely. I felt unsure, confused. But I was clear about one thing. Down there, the way he wanted to take us, was fire.

"No, wait." I pulled back, but he wouldn't release my arm. Instead of going down those steps, I knew that we needed to stay on the deck, skirt around the house, and move out onto the road. But he was leading us down into the fire. No, that was wrong. I knew that much.

He kept pulling. It was time to make him release. I let go of Alice and used that freed hand to grab onto my other fist whose wrist the firefighter was pinching in a tight lock. With one swift yank, I jerked my wrist free through the weak spot of his thumb. It was an easy release. Any beginner could do the simple self-defense trick if they pulled in the right spot, against the thumb. My force upset the balance of his momentum, and he stumbled a couple of steps before turning toward me. It was Dominic LePuc.

"You!" I said, blinking to clear my vision. "You're not a firefighter. What are you doing here?"

He didn't respond.

Somehow, I didn't think he and Jackson and Kingsley were all neighbors. Nor was he a volunteer firefighter. Goosebumps skittered across my flesh. Understanding swept through me in a flash. He whipped something out of a pocket and held it in front of him. A gun?

Firelight glinted off a blade, not a gun. I'd done the drill enough. Even sluggish, I knew to move when the warning screamed in my head. In half a second I tensed every muscle in my body, ready to leap to whichever side I needed for escape.

Footwork, my master sensei's voice nagged in my head. *Stay loose!*

An instant shot of adrenaline made me spring on my feet, uprooting myself from the solid deck boards. Instantly, I slid out of line of Dominic's aim.

He turned, treading heavily, following my direction. Leading him away from where Alice hunkered, I continued to bounce lightly on my feet, loosening my knees to weave this way and that. My stockinged feet gave me slippery traction, but I would have to deal with it. I heard a snarl of frustration when Dominic slipped. Better him than me.

I needed to learn to block better, that's what Master Hwang had said. My mind fuzzed over again. I needed a weapon.

He lunged again, and again I dodged him. Luckily, I'd trained on Master Hwang's heavy bag.

Footwork! Master Hwang had said. I danced and pranced on the balls of my feet, darting first one way and then another. Toward the wall of glass behind me, then toward Alice in her corner by the railing, then toward the wrap-around portion of the deck on the driveway side. I could've turned tail and escaped him that way, since I gambled that he wouldn't toss his knife, hoping to hit me like a dart. He might. But I wouldn't leave Alice behind.

Then I remembered my practice chuks in my bag, slung across my shoulder. The flails were only rubber, but they would still sting him. Besides, I didn't have anything else.

This wasn't demo practice. Not a test for Master Hwang, nor a tournament competition for a trophy. This was for real. I yanked the fake weapon out of my bag, tossed the bag aside, then shifted my weight evenly on the balls of my feet. Gripping the squishy flails, one in each hand, I held the rubber chuks in front of me like dangling udders.

My action surprised him enough to make him hesitate. He chuckled softly at me. "Idiot."

Exactly. But finesse was my friend. "What have you done to Alice?"

"She cannot help you now. Do not worry. I will take care of her after I'm done with you."

My fingers tightened around the rubber grips, and renewed

strength flowed through me like an elixir. "Why did you kill them?"

Distract him. Pull him off guard.

"Why?" He mimicked my voice, then laughed again, and his voice carried a sound of glee, of triumph, of absolute certainty of his own prowess. "For money, why else?"

So he did *kill them.* Ice clogged my adrenaline. "Alice has no money."

"She took *my* money."

"The cash in the firebox Jackson was looking for? Is that why you killed him?"

"If I tell you I'll have to kill *you*."

He stabbed at the air with his knife, and I leapt to one side, an example of Master Hwang's footwork. Dominic didn't have to tell me. I knew I was right.

"It's all for this, isn't it? You're growing yourself a cash crop here on Jackson's property." I was breathing heavily and trying my best not to let him hear my ragged gasps.

"Shut up and stop tiring yourself out. You think you're smart, but you can't get away."

"You're the one who can't get away. The fire department will be here any minute. Give yourself up, Dominic. It'll go easier for you if you turn yourself in."

"*Moi?* A world-renowned chef? Never."

"I've got news for you. Your world is a pretty small pond. Why would you risk everything for a cash crop?"

"What better place than here?"

I'd heard that before. Chief Niwot's curse had brought Alice back to Boulder. The lure of the mountains had made Kingsley stay, in spite of threatening poverty. And now, legalized marijuana had been too tempting for the likes of Dominic and his partners to resist cashing in on the cash crop.

Was Max one of his partners? My footwork tripped me up at the thought. Dominic must've caught my hesitation, for he lunged forward at that very moment, slicing a gash in my forearm.

Pain like fire seared through me, and I gasped, cried out, and fell backwards. I crashed against the glass window, rattling it, shattering the glass into thousands of splinters. Dominic kept coming with a wicked grin stretching across his face.

I slumped to the floor of the deck. Down, but not done. It was just a nick in my arm.

Never. Give. Up. Never!

Persistence—more than flashy karate talent—had seen me through my black belt test. Tenacity had given me my job, my best friend, and had brought me here to this moment, not knowing when to give up.

But Dominic didn't know that.

"Stupid broad," he said with a snicker and one step closer, as if checking to see if I was dead yet. Fire raged behind him, and glass crackled beneath his feet. He stopped. "Get in my way, will you? No one, not you, not Felix, no one will cheat me out of what is mine, do you hear?"

At the sound of the venom in his voice, adrenaline coursed through me like rocket fuel. The difficulty would come in restraining myself from killing him. One more step, and he would be close enough.

"You set that fire at Alice's house," I said, crumpled on my butt.

"It was a magnificent display."

He'd been there, at Alice's, admiring his handiwork. I'd seen him on the street, in the crowd, "helping" with crowd control. But really, he'd been gloating, unable to resist his arsonist's work. A mistake on his part.

"You thought Felix was cheating you."

"No one cheats *moi*, the great chef."

"Did you poison Felix, too?"

"That way, he could not resist."

"You can't get away. The firefighters will be here any minute."

"They are too late. I've already harvested, and the rest of the crop is torched, including you."

"The rain will put it out."

"That's what you think. It's not enough, and the ground is too dry this time of year. They will think lightning struck here, not my torch. As lightning will strike you and Alice."

"It's not worth it."

"*Au contraire*. Money, she is worth everything." He took another step.

I rolled to one side and flipped onto my feet, a bass-ackward version of Master Hwang's roll out of his head-standing position. I came up twirling the chuks, one in each hand, flinging droplets of my blood and splinters of broken glass everywhere as the rubber udders spun. I must've surprised him with my ninja turtle moves, and he stumbled backwards.

But backwards was what I wanted. Pulling him off guard gave me the opportunity I was waiting for. I lunged forward, sliding into a front leg front kick with the aid of my slippery socks, and all the while one twirling arm blocked as the other arced down, toward his knife-wielding arm. Chuk udders caught his wrist and wrapped around it. Only rubber, but the thrust was enough to knock the blade from his grip.

"Ha-saaaaa!" I shouted as I spun around, shooting out a sidekick that sent him plunging over the edge of the deck railing.

Twenty-One

WE WERE STILL talking about it two weeks later at the safety demo.

One of the local private schools had invited my martial arts studio to participate, demonstrating self-defense techniques at the beginning of their academic school year. The sponsors had arranged the demo to be held in a city park tucked up against the backdrop of mountains, where dogs took their guardians for walks and hang-gliders landed in open fields.

I was a sight, a shining example of having failed the self-defense issues I advocated. My arm was bandaged and the mottled circle of flesh had faded to an ugly yellow around my eye (yes, the nose pop *did* turn into a black eye after all). But actually I hadn't failed. Bottom line, I was alive.

I tried to stay out of sight as I watched Chanel organize Elliott and the rest of my students up there on the bandstand. They knew the drills. I'd trained them well.

Alice had brought a quilted blanket and a picnic basket filled with cucumber sandwiches, thanks to Pearle Pittman and her overabundant vegetable garden. Our old-lady neighbor had been fussing over me ever since that afternoon when she'd told me about birds and her friend, Alice's companion. I brought a cooler of lemonade—no tea for me for a while, thank you very much. We spread out on the grass and watched my students pair off and go through their drills. One of the pair threw punches, kicks, and aggressive grabs, while the other demoed how to block and release.

Their simulated fights tickled my still raw nerves.

"Thanks for coming today," I said to Alice. "How are you feeling?"

"You mean because of my trip to the hospital, or because of Jack?"

"Both, I guess. You didn't have to come today, but I'm glad you did."

"I'm okay. Really. Jack was fun, and I'm sorry he's gone, and yes, he was my boyfriend. There, I said it."

I patted her arm. "Why didn't you tell me that you were seeing someone?" I still couldn't believe I hadn't known, but then, she and I hadn't been friends all that long. We were still learning about each other. One day over margaritas, maybe I'd tell her about Max.

"After California," Alice said, "I was reluctant to get involved with anyone again. But I guess I was never all that serious about Jack. Anyway, I'll live. Luckily, I have experience starting over." She laughed, but tears glistened in the corners of her eyes.

"Yeah, me too."

We sat in companionable silence, tilting our faces up, letting the breeze catch our hair. Magpies squawked nearby, as if in response to the enthusiastic karate yells of my students. Bicyclists streamed by, pivoting their helmeted heads toward the demo under the roof of the bandstand.

"I know what Erica thinks about me," Alice said, her voice lowered, "but she's wrong. I didn't steal her husband."

"I know that."

"Come on, you can't know. That was before you and I ever met."

"Doesn't matter. I know what's in your heart. I know you're not that kind of person."

Alice sighed. "I took painting lessons from him when I first moved here, and I thought...I dunno."

"He walked on water?"

She laughed. "Yeah, maybe. He had that kind of influence over his students, even though his critiques could be tough to take. I knew he was going through a rough time with his marriage breaking up, and I had the right kind of space for his studio. Besides, I needed the rent money, so I thought why not invite him? I guess Erica took it the wrong way."

"She said you and Felix met in cooking class."

"Not true. I already knew him from painting. That's where I heard about the cooking classes. Truth is, I'm just not much of a cook."

A new thought flitted through my mind. "While you were there, did you ever meet..."

She lifted her eyebrows, waiting for me to go on, but I couldn't. "Meet who?"

"Nobody." I waved a bee away from my face. *Max*, I'd meant. But Max was history, and there was no point mucking through it all again.

Alice studied me thoughtfully, as if she could read my mind, and then like the good friend that she was, she changed the subject. "So now I've inherited a cat."

"You're her new guardian."

We laughed, and then she said, "I'm sorry about what Erica

did to your car."

I shrugged. "It's only paint." Anyway, I kind of liked being the b-lady.

"Well, she scared the bejeezus out of me," Alice said. "When that detective told me that Felix had died in the fire, I thought Erica must've set it, trying to kill me. I'm the one she had her quarrel with, after all, but the police didn't take me seriously. I was afraid that she'd keep trying and end up hurting either you or Terra. That's why I disappeared. I'm sorry I worried you, but I was afraid that if I phoned, you'd figure out where I was. I just couldn't take the chance."

"It all turned out okay in the end. Did you happen to notice that For Sale sign on Erica's front lawn?"

"Seriously? Such a loss for our neighborhood."

"Jimmie Condo will get his chance now." I reached for a sandwich with my bandaged arm and snickered, wondering who would get the better of whom. Where would it all end up? Condo… Cucumbers… Pearle had so many cucumbers that she'd asked Dad to help her stake them up to a trellis.

"Speaking of chance," Alice said, "how'd you know to go up there to Jack's place when I needed you the most?"

"I didn't. Dominic wanted me up there, so he could get rid of me. He forged a note from my ex that I couldn't ignore. Good thing I didn't drink all of my tea. Dominic must've poisoned it."

"As he poisoned the so-called gourmet dessert he wanted me to sample. A new creation, he called it. For one of his classes."

I shuddered. "Scary thought, his teaching people how to cook."

"Exactly," Alice said. "He claimed Jack had invited him up there to use his new kitchen and see how wonderful it was."

"And Robinette sampled it, too, in his test kitchen, poor

thing. How's she taking all this?" I scanned the other blankets of picnickers. "I thought she would've come today to watch her brother perform."

"She's got a new job. Delivering pizza."

A tandem bicycle wheeled up to a stop on the sidewalk next to our patch of grass. A lithe woman in stretchy shorts swung off from the back seat, undid her helmet, and shook out her blonde hair. Gillian! She clogged over to me in her spiked shoes while her partner—a man, of course—chained the bike to a rack.

"*Here* you are," she said breathlessly, turning her back on my students.

"Since when have you taken up bicycling?" I asked, nodding at her partner at the rack.

"Since meeting Sean, of course."

"Sean? What happened to Jimmie Condo?"

"Don't be silly. Jimmie is no fun. He would never be caught dead on a bicycle, not like Sean."

"Sean?"

"I think you know him. Sean Hennesey."

"*Detective* Hennesey?"

"Right. You should keep an open mind, Nell. Sean is not just a cop. He's a pro bicycle racer."

I choked on my lemonade about the time that the detective approached, releasing his mat of hair from under his helmet.

"Ladies," he said with a nod at Alice and me. Then he encircled Gillian's waist with one arm. "Once again, Ms. Letterly, we are indebted to you."

Good thing I was already sitting, because I would've fallen over for sure. "Who's 'we'? You and Jill? Or you and the police?"

"Oh, Nell, stop it," Gillian said. "Of course you're a hero.

Have you seen yourself in the mirror? You're covered with battle scars."

Alice giggled.

"Then, maybe you'll explain a few things I still don't understand." I was staring at his arm around my sister-in-law.

"Go ahead, shoot."

"I know Dominic and Felix partnered together to grow more marijuana than what the law allows for private consumption, and I know they went in together to sell it without a license, but what I don't get is *why*. Why would they risk everything? Their careers and their reputations and their families? And all for a pitiful amount of cash."

The lines on Hennesey's suntanned face hardened, making him look more like a detective and less like a cyclist. "It was a substantial amount of cash, not pitiful at all. They were just another pair of opportunists, and together, they made a perfect storm. Luckily, they are out of business now, and Dominic LePuc is off the streets, thanks to you."

I hadn't hurt him with my kick. Not seriously, that is. His fall off the deck had left him lying there on the ground, winded long enough for me to find some twine in the kitchen to tie him up. It held him good enough until the authorities arrived and took him into custody.

"Don't you get it?" Gillian said, squinting into the sun. "Felix was always good at gardening, and he used those skills to grow the crop on Jackson's land, who in turn received a cut of the profits. Then Felix dried the plants in his attic, and Dominic used his chef skills to make the edibles they sold."

"I didn't know there was anything in them," Alice said, earnestness lifting her voice. "Robinette helped me in the store, and she brought the candies in from her dad. Called them 'meditation mints.' I trusted her! She worked for me, after all. How could I know there was anything wrong with her mints?"

"It's okay, honey." I rubbed Alice's back.

"They made more from selling weed on the streets," Gillian explained, "than from the edibles. With recreational marijuana legalized, pot is less available on the streets, but there is still a large market. It was more profitable for them to sell illegally than with a license. Now do you understand how it works?"

Oh boy. I had an inkling that my soon-to-be-ex sister-in-law was going to become insufferable as long as she continued her relationship with the detective. "That still doesn't explain *why*." My voice came out sounding as grumbly as Dad's.

Gillian went on. "Well you see, Dominic thought that Felix was cheating him out of the profits that they kept in the fireproof box —"

"There was nothing in it," Alice said.

"What?" We all turned to look at Alice.

"Nothing," she repeated. "If there had been any money, it would've been mine, for all the back rent Felix owed me. I was so angry when I found the box empty that I just left and walked around a while, letting off steam. I told you I went to the movies, but I didn't."

"I can confirm that," Hennesey said. "We confiscated the box at the fire site, and it was empty. Maybe Dominic was right, and Felix really was cheating him."

"You think Felix spent the money?" I said.

Hennesey shrugged, and Alice's face steamed as if she'd eaten a pepper instead of a cucumber.

"But if the box was empty all along," I said, "then Jackson had nothing to fear. And he was plenty scared. He thought whoever was after that box must've thought he had the money. He was running for his life when he smashed into those trashcans in the alley, and then Dominic caught up to him with his knife." I turned to Hennesey and asked, "Did Dominic ever confess about that?"

Hennesey's jaw clamped. "I am not privileged to say at the moment."

"Aw, honey-bunny." Gillian flicked her fingernails across the back of his neck.

Hennesey's Adam's apple moved, but his lips did not.

"Never mind," I said. "It's obvious, isn't it? Jack died from a knife wound. It had to be Dominic who did it. I'll bet Dominic slashed Jack's tire, and that's what made Jack lose control when he tried to drive away. Dominic was waiting for him with his knife."

"Interesting speculation," Hennesey said, "but you really need to keep that opinion to yourself."

"Yes sir." I fought a smile. I knew I was right.

A jingle of tags startled me as a loose dog dove onto our blanket, sniffing the basket of sandwiches and upsetting a cup of lemonade.

"Bruno!" A man's voice called from the distance, and the dog leapt away.

Alice mopped up the lemonade spill, and I rose on unsteady feet. I hadn't seen Kingsley since he'd driven me down from the mountains, and now here he was, jogging out from behind a group of hikers.

"I didn't expect to see you again." My grin stretched wider.

"You can never get too many safety tips," he said, watching

my students on the bandstand.

"Especially when you're in the extermination business."

"Actually, that's what brings me around. You remember that unpaid bill we were discussing?"

"For 'services rendered'?"

"That's the one."

"Did you finally receive payment?" He was telling me that he'd finally caught up with Max. I was sure that's what he meant. My heart did a flip. Max *was* in town. Kingsley had found him.

He shook his head. "I'm taking it off the books. Your neighbor confessed that she'd had one drink too many when she thought the person of interest might be in a position to pay up. She made a mistake. Your man was never here in town after all."

"He's not *my* man," I said with a growl. "And what about the blondes?"

"No man, no blondes."

"What man?" Gillian said, staring pointedly at Kingsley's hairy legs. "What blondes?" She curled a lock of her blonde hair around one finger. "What are you two talking about? You should remember your manners, Nell, and introduce us."

"Oh, right," I said. "This is, uh, Kin —"

"Kenny," Kingsley said. "An old college friend. Just moved back to town. Here to tell you I ran into another mutual friend: Celeste. She sends her regards and a message. She couldn't be here because she and her husband just left on a cruise. Her husband remembered he really loves her, so he forgave her. She remembered she loves his money. So they're on a second honeymoon. But don't worry. They'll be back."

I wasn't worried. "As in Chief Niwot's curse," I said with a snort. His curse kept bringing everyone back to Boulder in the end.

Alice slapped her forehead. "Now I know what I'm going to paint for you, Nell, like I promised to do. Chief Niwot. What do you think?"

"Nice," I said, not telling her what I thought. Heaven help us if the chief *really* brought Max back one day.

* * * * *

Nell Letterly's Self Defense Tips

Sometimes amateur sleuthing will land you in trouble. If, like Nell, you are a magnet for trouble, then here's a review of five basic safety tips from *Murder for a Cash Crop*:

1. Avoid trouble: The best defense in martial arts is not to have to use any defense techniques at all. Don't deliberately antagonize angry people. And above all, stay away from bears. You're better off without a selfie of yourself with a bear. Never get between a bear and a trash can, nor between a mama bear and its cubs.

2. Strangers: Never invite a stranger into your car, nor into your house. If you believe you're a target, then check under your car before opening the car door.

If avoidance isn't possible, and you find yourself cornered:

3. Stay light on your feet: Shift your weight evenly onto the balls of your feet so that you can run away fast in any direction that opens up. You won't know which way you may need to escape.

4. Car chases: If someone follows you in your car, lead them to the police station. And if your car starts to skid along the way, remember to steer in the opposite direction of the way the nose of the car tries to point.

If someone grabs you by the arm:

5. Release that grip! Pull your arm in the direction of the assailant's thumb. A thug's thumb is never strong enough to hold you one-handed.

Good luck, have fun, and remember to stay safe!

About the Author

Sue Star writes mysteries about families in chaos. She is the author of the Nell Letterly mystery series. Like her character, Sue has also trained and taught the martial arts, but unlike her character, Sue believes her life is more stable. She enjoys hiking, traveling, and just hanging out with her family.

Sue also writes stand-alone short mystery stories and has collected several in *Trophy Hunting* and *Organized Death*. *Trouble in a Politically Correct Town* contains stories about Nell Letterly's friends. Sue is currently hard at work on the fourth novel in the series, tentatively called *Murder by Moose*.

Find out more about her writing at dmkregpublishing.com

Follow Sue on facebook, twitter and goodreads.

Contact Sue at suestarauthor@gmail.com

Need Another
Sue Star
Fix?

The Nell Letterly Mystery Series: Available **now** from your favorite bookstore in trade paper or e-book format:

> *Murder in the Dojo* (#1) Nell's first day on the job at the dojo turns deadly.
>
> *Murder with Altitude* (#2) Training for the local 10-k run turns deadly.
>
> *Murder by Moose* (#4) Coming in 2017. Autumn treks in high-mountain meadows turn deadly.

Sue's short story collections: Available **now** in e-book format on all the e-reader platforms:

> *Trouble in a Politically Correct Town:* Three stories about Nell Letterly's friends. A selection on the next page.
>
> *Organized Death*: Even the most organized women stumble when a crime occurs.
>
> *Trophy Hunting*: Trophies come in all forms.

Read selections of all at: www.dmkregpublishing.com

Following is an excerpt from "Creek Squatting," a short story in ***Trouble in a Politically Correct Town***, stories about Nell Letterly's friends

from

Sue Star

Available in June 2016 from D.M. Kreg Publishing

Sean Hennesey spotted the shoe during his routine patrol along Boulder's creek path. Morning sun bounced off one of the rocks in the creek, giving the rock an unusual light plain. That's what made him notice. Such dramatic shifts in value always yanked his attention, especially during patrol. He had to stay sharp.

A shoe wedged there, messing with the pattern of light. Some tuber must've lost a tennis shoe. Tubing was banned this week due to heavy run-off from snowmelt. He propped his department-issue bike against a cottonwood and rustled through the underbrush to the creek's edge, to get a closer look.

A body attached to the shoe. The body—looked like a man—was mostly submerged beneath tumbling water. Hennesey called dispatch for back-up. There would be no painting breaks for him today.

Seeking an explanation, he glanced up at the mountain backdrop. Sunrise blended cadmium yellows and oranges on the snow banks up there, where run-off started. Melting snow gushed down the mountainside and eventually slammed into the edge of town at the mouth of the canyon. The swollen creek pounded through the middle of town, all the way here, to where Hennesey stood on Boulder's eastern extremity.

The victim could've fallen in anywhere along that route and been tossed along with the current. Or he could've fallen in right here, losing his balance, getting his shoe wedged between rocks. It wouldn't take long for the icy water to numb him.

Had someone helped him lose his balance? This part of the creek path was more isolated than the rest.

Hennesey retraced his steps, not wanting to contaminate a possible crime scene any more than he already had. It wasn't likely this was a crime scene—this was peaceful Boulder, after all, and the university wasn't in session at the moment—but still he couldn't afford mistakes. He was a rookie.

Finally he could hear the distant wailing of sirens. Back-up, on its way. About the same time, he saw a woman's face peering at him from behind the bushes that lined the cement walk.

"Ma'am, would you kindly step out here onto the path, please?"

"Me? But I haven't done anything." A smoker's cough hacked through her.

"I would like to ask you a few questions, ma'am."

"I don't have a lawyer!"

"What is your name, ma'am, and where do you live?"

Stepping out from behind her bush, she gripped a big black inner tube, like the kinds that were banned right now on the rushing, swirling creek. "They call me Rainbow," she said.

www.ingramcontent.com/pod-product-compliance
Lightning Source LLC
Chambersburg PA
CBHW071311250626
47159CB00004B/1382